Christmas Gift (Christian Romance, Religious Fiction Romance)

Kathleen Wiseman

Christmas Gift (Christian Romance / Religious Fiction Romance)
© Copyright by Kathleen Wiseman 2012.
First edition
All rights reserved.
ISBN 9781480215467
All rights reserved under International Copyright Law.
No part of this book may be stored or reproduced in any form without the express written permission of the copyright holder.

Edited by Divine Grace Editing

Twitter
http://twitter.com/CleanRomanceBks

Pinterest:
http://pinterest.com/kathleenwiseman

Website: http://christianwomensfiction.com

Facebook
https://www.facebook.com/KathleenWisemanChristianRomanceAuthor

This book may contain references to specific commercial products, process or service by trade name, trademark, manufacturer, or otherwise, specific brand-name products and/or trade names of products, which are trademarks or registered trademarks and/or trade names, and these are property of their respective owners. Kathleen Wiseman, her publishers and associates have no association with any specific commercial products, process or service by trade name, trademark, manufacturer, or otherwise, specific brand-name products and/or trade names of products.

This is a work of fiction. Any resemblance to any person, living or dead, is purely coincidental. The personal names have been invented by the author, and any likeness to the name of any person, living or dead, is purely coincidental.

And God said, Let the waters bring forth abundantly the moving creature that hath life, and fowl [that] may fly above the earth in the open firmament of heaven.
And God created great whales, and every living creature that moveth, which the waters brought forth abundantly, after their kind, and every winged fowl after his kind: and God saw that [it was] good.
And God blessed them, saying, Be fruitful, and multiply, and fill the waters in the seas, and let fowl multiply in the earth.
And the evening and the morning were the fifth day.
And God said, Let the earth bring forth the living creature after his kind, cattle, and creeping thing, and beast of the earth after his kind: and it was so.
And God made the beast of the earth after his kind, and cattle after their kind, and every thing that creepeth upon the earth after his kind: and God saw that [it was] good.
(Genesis 1:20-25)

* * * * * * * * * * * * * * * * *

Are not five sparrows sold for two farthings, and not one of them is forgotten before God?

But even the very hairs of your head are all numbered. Fear not therefore: ye are of more value than many sparrows.

Also I say unto you, Whosoever shall confess me before men, him shall the Son of man also confess before the angels of God.

(Luke 12:6-8.)

The LORD shall preserve thee from all evil: he shall preserve thy soul. The LORD shall preserve thy going out and thy coming in from this time forth, and even for evermore.
(Psalm 121:7-8)

Chapter One.

Rachel handed the blue and cream, bicolor Persian cat over to the veterinary nurse, and then sighed. "I'm going to miss this place."

The nurse laughed. "Come on, I know you've always wanted to work with horses and the closest we get to a horse is a Great Dane. Besides, you'll be back in six months. I'm surprised you worked in a small animal practice to start with."

Rachel sighed again. "Look at me, straight from college, and who would give a short, skinny girl like me a job wrestling with cattle and horses?"

The nurse looked at Rachel's small, feminine, petite frame and nodded. "S'pose it doesn't help that you're so pale with long blonde hair. If someone didn't know you, they'd think you were fragile. You *are* an awfully good vet, though."

Rachel smiled her thanks just as the next patient entered, a small, yapping Maltese Terrier with a seemingly endless array of sharp teeth. "I'd rather deal with a big steer than a little, spoiled dog," Rachel said under her breath to the nurse, as the client fussed over the little dog which snapped constantly at Rachel.

"Where is the vet?" the elderly woman demanded.

"I *am* the vet." Rachel was tired of people assuming she was not a vet just because she was a woman, all five feet two inches of her. What century was this? Her tone must have been too fervent, as the woman said no more and the nurse raised her eyebrows in amusement.

After the Maltese Terrier, Rachel took a moment to eat a sandwich in the small, drab kitchen which doubled as an office. The Paws and Claws Pet Hospital was not flush with funds, but made do as best it could. On the other hand, her old family friend Liam Mariner assured her that the Wild Oak Animal Clinic, at which she would spend Christmas, and then another few months, was well funded and had the very latest equipment. What's more, it was a large animal practice which was just what Rachel wanted.

Rachel was struck with a moment's disquiet. Was she doing the right thing in accepting the temporary position in her home town? Rachel had been close to her father, but had a rocky relationship with her mother and sister, both of whom were annoyed that Rachel was a Christian like her father had been. Rachel's mother had insisted that Rachel come home this Christmas, as Rachel had somehow managed to avoid spending Christmas with her family after her father had gone home to be with the Lord. Liam's suggestion that she fill in for him at short notice had indeed seemed a Godsend; working over Christmas would mean she would not be forced to spend every available hour with her mother and sister but would nevertheless be home for Christmas.

As a bird that wandereth from her nest, so [is] a man that wandereth from his place.
(Proverbs 27:8)

Chapter Two.

Although she did not start until the following week, Rachel decided to drive past the Wild Oak Animal Clinic on her way to her childhood home. Gone was the little brick building she remembered; in its place was a large modern building with plenty of dark glass which reminded her of a sleek, modern day cathedral. It was not huge by big city standards but nevertheless the whole impression was one of up-market sophistication. It was all more than a little intimidating, especially after the modest renovated cottage - turned veterinary hospital where Rachel had worked since college.

Snow was everywhere. Rachel had missed the snow, having worked in Florida since college. Snow always brought back happy memories of her father and her carefree childhood.

Rachel drove through town carefully, as she had grown unaccustomed to driving in such weather conditions, noting that not much else had seemed to change in her absence. As she drove up the gravel driveway to the farm house, her anxiety grew. Other people generally loved Christmas, but to

Rachel it had always been a source of tension. Rather, any family get-together had proven a source of tension.

Rachel's mother, Carole, was sitting on the porch when Rachel drove up. The covered front porch, made of white-washed pine, ran the length of the house except for the double garage to its right. Rachel and her mother greeted each other warmly; family reunions were usually off to a good start. It was only after a few hours that the remarks would start.

"Where's Dinah?"

"Your sister's inside." Carole took Rachel by the arm and led her into the living room where the fireplace was glowing.

The knotty pine, vaulted ceilings throughout the home coupled with the open plan design should have offered a relaxing ambience, but even now Rachel was only too aware of the tension bubbling under the surface.

"Come and sit by the fire, Rachel. I'll call Dinah."

Dinah appeared at that very moment. Dinah was unlike Rachel in most ways. Whereas Rachel was petite and blonde, Dinah was tall, brunette, and curvy.

"Is that cat hair on you, Rachel?" Dinah asked by way of greeting. "You know I'm allergic."

"Hello to you too. No, I can't see how it could be."

"Have you just come from work?" Dinah looked Rachel up and down, leaving Rachel feeling self conscious, as always, in Dinah's presence.

"No, of course not. I always wear jeans." Rachel noted that Dinah, in a snugly fitting dress, looked overdressed for just sitting around the house. Her elegant sandals looked more beautiful thanks to the glistening toenail polish, which matched the polish on her perfectly manicured hands.

"Wine?"

"No thanks, but I'd love a coffee."

"You still don't drink?" It sounded like an accusation.

"No."

Dinah snorted rudely. "Jesus' first miracle was turning water into wine, wasn't it?"

Here we go.

"I'm not saying you shouldn't drink, Dinah. It's just that I don't. I don't want a big issue over it."

Dinah pretended to look shocked. "An issue? Whatever do you mean? I see you're still overly sensitive like you always were. Come on, I'll make you a coffee. Do you have a boyfriend?"

Rachel was thrown by the sudden change in subject. "No, do you?"

"Not at the moment, but at least I've had several. Be careful or one day you'll end up an old maid with a lot of cats, wondering where your life went."

Rachel bit her tongue, and followed Dinah into the kitchen. As Dinah put on the coffee pot, Rachel walked over to the window which overlooked the woods. Now that it was winter, the leaves were off the trees and so the river could be seen. As a child, Rachel had loved to see the bald eagles perching in the imposing cotton wood trees behind the river. Rachel's father had loved all animals, but not so her mother or sister. They were kind to animals, but considered them a nuisance and a waste of money. When Rachel's father passed away, her mother sold off all the land with the exception of the portion around the house, and sold every horse.

Rachel and Dinah carried their coffee back to the fireplace, where Carole, their mother, was sitting. The rest of the afternoon was spent making small talk about babies and biological clocks, interspersed with anecdotes of bratty things Rachel was supposed to have done as a child.

Two more days, Rachel thought, *I have to endure two more days of this, then I start work. I hope I'm on call seven days a week.*

And out of the ground the LORD God formed every beast of the field, and every fowl of the air; and brought [them] unto Adam to see what he would call them: and whatsoever Adam called every living creature, that [was] the name thereof.
(Genesis 2:19)

Chapter Three.

If Rachel had expected a warm welcome, she was wrong. Her new employer was civil and polite, but cold, and he left her in no doubt that he considered her to be most unsuitable for the position.

"This is a large animal practice, you know. We do farm animals as well as pets. I was expecting Liam's temporary replacement to be a horse or cattle veterinarian, not someone from a city practice only used to dogs and cats." Dr. Scott Miller almost spat the words, *dogs and cats*.

Rachel was indignant. "That position was offered to me straight from college and I *am* used to cattle and horses. My family bred and showed Quarter Horses 'til my father passed away a few years ago and he did show Santa Gertrudis cattle as well."

Dr. Miller snorted. "Yes, Liam told me after he'd offered you the position. I don't wish to be rude, but I know he's an old friend of your family's. Favors are one thing, but I'm responsible for the welfare of animals, and I did need someone who is very experienced in large animal medicine, not a slip of a girl."

Rachel's furious retort died on her tongue as a veterinary nurse called urgently to Dr. Miller. She looked around his office wondering what to do next. *Coming home was a mistake, for sure*, she said to herself. *If Liam didn't own half this business, no doubt I'd be fired already.*

Rachel didn't know what to do. *Do I sit here, or leave?* She decided to remain, and figured Dr. Miller would eventually return with instructions for her.

Rachel looked around the office. It was cold, like Dr. Miller, but also like Dr. Miller, it was very attractive. Light flooded through the open windows, making the industrial cable lighting unnecessary, at least at this time of day. Dark patterned, timber cupboards presumably hid paperwork, as the room was totally deficient of clutter, or indeed any sign of daily work. There were even no shelving units. An antique, unusually carved, solid oak partner's desk complete with green leather inset dominated the room. Rachel thought the fluted legs in the French neoclassical style rather too feminine a choice for such a masculine man, and wondered if a wife had chosen it for him. The duck egg, blue and white color scheme also suggested a feminine touch.

The room was nevertheless devoid of family photos. Her last employer had photos of his wife and children all over his office.

He probably doesn't have a wife; although he's attractive, he's so unpleasant, Rachel thought.

He did however have photos of two cats, two dogs, and a large framed photo of him on a horse, obviously at a Three Day Event competition, on the wall to the side of his desk.

He does have a good seat on a horse, Rachel thought, and walked over to study the photo more closely.

Just then Dr. Miller poked his head around the door. "I have to leave, but come on, I'll introduce you to everyone first."

Rachel interrupted. "Do you have time to tell me my duties, Dr. Miller?"

Dr. Miller looked flustered. "Call me Scott; we're all on a first-name basis here. Err, duties." He rubbed his forehead. "You can be back-up for Paul in surgery today. We're fully booked, mainly dew-claws, spaying, vaccinating, that sort of thing."

Great. Dogs and cats. I wonder if he'll ever let me near a farm animal? This is off to a bad start. Rachel was dejected, but she had no time to brood as Scott was introducing her to everyone.

"This is Paul, one of our vets. Kenneth is out on a call with one of our nurses, Teresa; you'll meet them later."

Rachel and Paul shook hands. Paul was an attractive man and in his forties, Rachel guessed.

"This is Paul's wife, Linda. She's our receptionist. This is Shirley who does the books. This is Cindy, one of our vet nurses, and Annette, also a vet nurse."

By the time Scott finished the introductions, Rachel's head was spinning. She was better with animals' names than people's. She was sure she'd soon forget everyone's name, if she hadn't already. She figured she'd remember Shirley's name as she was much older than everyone else, and Rachel's first cat had been named Shirley.

To Rachel's relief, Paul took her under his wing and the morning was spent on routine matters. Everyone, both staff and clients, seemed friendly, and although there was no doubt office politics, there was no sign of any such thing so far. It was soon time for lunch, and Rachel and the nurse Annette ate in the staff room, a far fancier version of the kitchen at her old clinic.

"Has anyone showed you around yet?"

When Rachel answered in the negative, Annette gave her a guided tour. There were kennels with indoor and outdoor runs, a barn with stalls, and in the main building, three examination rooms, and for the staff, the large staff room, and both a male bathroom and a female bathroom with showers.

"What do you think of Scott?"

Rachel tried to think of something polite to say, and could not, so fielded the question. "This place has changed so much since I left. Our family used to call out Liam to our animals, and then I heard that he'd sold half a share in the practice to Scott."

"He's attractive, isn't he?"

"Liam? Um, well.."

Annette laughed. "No, Scott of course."

"Well, yes, I suppose." Rachel recalled his tall athletic frame, his broad shoulders, his thick, chocolate colored hair and piercing brown eyes, and what's more, she recalled how the treacherous butterflies in her stomach had set off in full flight at the first sight of him.

Annette was still speaking. "He'd be a good catch for someone."

"He's not married?"

"No."

Rachel thought she saw a glint in Annette's eye. Perhaps Annette had a little crush on the boss.

Annette pressed on. "Are you married?"

Rachel shook her head.

"Boyfriend?" Annette fixed her eyes on Rachel. The question sounded insistent.

"No. What about you?" Rachel attempted to turn the questioning back onto Annette.

"I'm working on it."

Rachel was saved from the uncomfortable conversation as Paul called her to the next patient, a big Rottweiler with a sore ear. Without thinking, Rachel picked up the dog easily and deposited her on the examination table.

Paul whistled. "Wow, Rachel, have you ever thought of entering a weight lifting competition?"

Both Rachel and the dog's owner laughed. "I've ridden horses for years; that and lifting horse feed builds up the muscles. I'm much stronger than I look."

"Clearly." Paul was amused.

Rachel enjoyed the rest of the afternoon, and at five p.m., Scott called her back into his office. He gestured her to the seat opposite his desk, then sat down, and picked up a pile of papers. "How was your day?" he asked, without looking up.

Rachel felt put out, but did not exactly know why. "Fine, thanks."

Scott looked up. "I mean, are you coping all right? Do you think you'll fit in? Did you run into any problems, and can you foresee any?"

Rachel took a deep breath. "The work was routine. I feel comfortable here; everyone is nice."

Scott nodded and then looked back down to shuffle his papers. "Paul mentioned that you're quite competent."

Rachel did not respond. When Scott did not speak either, she asked, "Do you think I could do some large animal work at some point, preferably soon? That's partly why I accepted Liam's offer. My goal is to work in a large animal clinic, specifically with horses."

Scott looked up, startled.

Anyone would think I'd just told him that little green men had landed, Rachel thought irritably.

"Um, well, we'll see. That will be all. See you tomorrow."

And with that, Rachel was dismissed from his office.

This is not going to be a very good Christmas, she thought.

How was she going to work closely with the cold, abrupt Dr. Scott Miller every day? Worse still, it was clear that he had no intention of letting her anywhere near a sheep or goat, much less an alpaca, and as for a horse, well she might as well forget that right away. All the staff members were friendly enough, although she'd only spoken to two or three of them so far.

Worse still, she had to go home to an overly critical mother and a haughty sister, both of whom liked to make jokes at her expense.

I wish I'd never come, she sighed to herself. *I think I'm going to have a miserable Christmas.*

*And thou shalt love the LORD thy God with all thine heart, and with all thy soul, and with all thy might.
And these words, which I command thee this day, shall be in thine heart: And thou shalt teach them diligently unto thy children, and shalt talk of them when thou sittest in thine house, and when thou walkest by the way, and when thou liest down, and when thou risest up.*
(Deuteronomy 6:5 -7)

Chapter Four.

The week did not improve, apart from the fact that after the first day, Rachel was allowed to see patients by herself, without Paul. It was just the same as the old clinic, only with far better and more up to date equipment. The days were spent on routine matters and Rachel was not even assigned any emergency cases. She was not even put on call, so left the clinic at five every afternoon, back to her mother and sister, who berated her, both openly and with little, underhanded remarks, about being so passionate about her work and working in what they called an "unladylike profession."

By Sunday, Rachel was looking forward to Church. While Rachel always looked forward to Church, this time she really needed to feel God's presence and worship Him away from the negative atmosphere of her mother's home, and the frustrating time at the veterinary clinic.

Rachel pulled into the parking lot and looked at the little, wooden church. It had not changed in her absence. The church was affectionately referred to as a "Bishop Whittle Church" in honor of Bishop Whittle, as were many wooden churches in the medieval gothic style built in the second half of the nineteen century in Minnesota.

This Church had been originally built as an Episcopal Church and in every way was a fine example of the medieval gothic revival in Church architecture, in particular with its emphasis on altar rather than on pulpit and small communion table. Rachel always felt a part of history when in this Church. In contrast, the Church she had attended since she had left college was spacious and contemporary with floor to ceiling windows, and a vast, clear skylight above the auditorium. Rachel loved attending night services and looking at the stars, in awe of God's mighty creation.

Rachel was a little nervous going back to the Church today, so was relieved to run into a familiar face no sooner than she had locked her car.

"Rachel! I didn't expect to see you here."

Rachel spun around. It was Shirley, the book keeper at the clinic.

"Hi Shirley."

"Are you a Christian?"

Rachel was a little taken aback by the abruptness of the question.

"Yes, definitely."

Shirley laughed. "Sorry, that must have sounded rude. It's lovely that there's another Christian at the clinic now. Are you here alone? You're not married, no boyfriend?"

"Yes, I'm here alone, and no on both counts, no husband or boyfriend." Rachel laughed too.

"You'll have to sit with me then. I always come alone."

Rachel detected sadness in Shirley's voice. "I've come here all my life, before I went to College," Rachel offered.

"I only moved to the area eighteen months ago," Shirley said.

Rachel and Shirley walked into the building. The usher smiled at Rachel, obviously trying to place her face. He handed the two women a service bulletin each. Several people smiled at Rachel, and some embraced her warmly and asked what she had been doing since they last saw her. Rachel felt quite at home. As they took their seats, Rachel turned to Shirley. "You don't have a husband or boyfriend either?"

Shirley looked so sad that Rachel felt bad for asking the question. "My husband passed away some years ago, and my son has fallen away. He won't hear a word about the Lord these days."

Rachel clasped the woman's hand and patted it. "You know what Proverbs chapter twenty two verse six says, 'Train up a child in the way he should go: and when he is old, he will not depart from it.'"

Shirley sighed deeply. "Yes, but many commentators say that particular Scripture means that if you brought up a child the right way, he would never depart from God. They say it doesn't mean that he will return to God at some later time. I obviously didn't bring him up the right way, although I thought I'd provided him with a good, Christian upbringing."

Rachel was at a loss, not knowing how to comfort Shirley.

Everyone stood for the first hymn, so no further conversation was possible.

Rachel was elated after the service; the cares and concerns of the last week had just melted away. The sermon had been uplifting and encouraging. People milled around Rachel, wanting to know her news, whether she was back to stay, and so on. Rachel noted that Shirley was an active member of the Church and everyone seemed to like her. As Rachel was about to leave, Shirley caught her arm.

"Would you like to come to dinner tonight? I understand if it's too short notice."

Rachel was delighted to have made a new friend, and a Christian friend at that. "I'd love to, thank you."

"Say, six?"

Rachel nodded. "That would be lovely."

Shirley wrote down the address on a slip of paper and handed it to Rachel. "Would you like me to write down directions?"

Rachel looked at the address. "Oh no, that's okay; I know where that street is. It's right in town."

Rachel drove away blissfully happy. The Church service had been wonderful, and she had made a new friend, not only a Christian, but what was more, a Christian friend from her work place. She was looking forward to dinner, ignoring the small feeling of warning that niggled at her.

Better [is] a dinner of herbs where love is, than a stalled ox and hatred therewith.
(Proverbs 15:17)

Chapter Five.

Rachel pulled into the snowy street and parked outside the classic two and a half story house complete with asphalt shingles peeping out from under the snow on the pitched roof.

It seems an awfully big house for just one person, Rachel thought, shivering against the blast of cold air and reaching back into the car for the cake she had made that afternoon.

Shirley was already waiting for her at the door to the covered porch. "Come in, come in, out of the cold. Oh dear, you didn't have to bring anything."

"It's a German Black Forest Cherry Christmas cake."

"That looks delicious. I'd love the recipe, if you wouldn't mind."

"Of course. It's an old recipe from my father's family," Rachel said as she stepped under cover, pleased to reach the warmth of the porch. "The temperature's so nice in here. I'll thaw out in no time."

"The house has forced-air heating." Shirley took the cake while Rachel took off her coat.

Rachel looked around the enclosed porch. Although the light was on, it seemed dark and a little gloomy, despite the white wicker furniture albeit covered with numerous navy blue cushions.

Shirley walked inside, presumably to put the cake in the kitchen, while Rachel followed her. As they walked through the dining room, Rachel admired the high, vaulted ceilings and only noticed at the last minute that the table was set for three.

I thought Shirley lived alone, she thought.

There was no sign of the third person in the kitchen. Rachel, who had a keen interest in interior design, thought the kitchen a little dated and oppressive with all the timber, although it was nevertheless enormous. The appliances were stainless steel and looked new, while the timber cupboards were yellowing, and the tiles had scenes of large fruit baskets.

Rachel heard footsteps and turned to see the person for whom the third place was set.

"You!"

Rachel was not sure whether she had said the word, or whether the man in front of her had uttered it, as she was so shocked to see him. It was clear that the shock was entirely mutual.

"What are you doing here?" Scott demanded.

Rachel just stared at him, taken aback both by the rude remark, and by the fact that she had not expected to see Scott Miller in Shirley's house.

"Scott, dear, that was rude." Turning to Rachel she said, "You'll have to forgive my son. He's better with animals than people."

Rachel was still struck speechless. *Shirley is Scott Miller's mother? I had no idea.*

"I apologize if I sounded rude." In spite of his words, Scott's tone held no apology. "Mom said she was bringing home a church friend for dinner; I had no idea it was you."

"I had no idea Shirley was your mother," Rachel countered. The two of them were standing opposite each other like two dogs with the hair on the back of their necks bristling.

Scott's face clearly showed his disbelief. "Oh come on now, I introduced Shirley as my mom when I introduced you to everyone at the clinic. Didn't you see my car in the driveway?"

Did he introduce Shirley as his mother? Rachel was unsure. *Surely I would have remembered that.* At any rate, Scott's impolite tone had Rachel's back up. "Why would I make that up?" she snapped. "I'm not in the habit of lying. Shirley didn't mention you once, the whole time at Church. I had no idea anyone else was coming for dinner. Besides, I have no idea what your car looks like as I've been in the clinic every day. I haven't been out assisting you."

Shirley spoke up. "Scott, you're being rude to my guest. Do you realize how you sounded?"

Scott for the first time looked contrite. "Sorry, Mom. I apologize, Rachel," he said for the second time, but this time Rachel figured he possibly meant it.

Rachel was furious that Scott appeared to think she had ulterior motives for accepting Shirley's invitation, but also felt bad for reacting to Scott in Shirley's home and thus potentially making things unpleasant for Shirley.

I'll have to make an effort not to let him get on my nerves for the rest of the night, she counseled herself. *He sure has tabs on himself. I bet he thought I wanted to be set up on a blind date with him. He's completely insufferable.*

The atmosphere between Scott and Rachel at the dinner table was awfully tense, although Shirley showed no sign that she noticed it. When Shirley left to bring in the main meal, refusing offers of help from both Scott and Rachel, the two of them sat in awkward silence. Rachel was pleased to see Shirley return.

It seemed like she was gone forever, she thought.

"I hope you like Buffalo Dry Rub Wings," Shirley said triumphantly, placing a large platter on the table.

"I do. I haven't had them for years." Rachel smiled at the memory.

"Let's say Grace now. Would like to say it, Scott?"

Rachel stole a glance at Scott who had turned beet-red and all but glared at his mother. "You say Grace, Mom."

Shirley lost no time. "Hold hands, everyone. Bless us, O Lord, and these Thy gifts, for which we are about to receive. Dear Father God, thank You for this meal and the fellowship and for blessing this household with peace, through Jesus Christ, our Lord. Amen."

Rachel said, "Amen," but noticed that Scott did not. He dropped Rachel's hand like a hot potato, which suited Rachel fine, as she had felt horribly uneasy holding Scott's hand and at the same time ill at ease due to the electric currents running through her at his touch.

Rachel felt bad for Shirley going to so much trouble to make a lovely dinner, and then have such tension between her guests, so asked about the recipe for Buffalo Dry Rub Wings.

Shirley beamed. "You can't forget the brown sugar and the blue cheese dressing. I just use the spices in the usual recipe: smoked paprika, hot cayenne pepper, chili, cumin, and garlic. Oh, is garlic a spice? Never mind, there's plenty of it in it."

"It's delicious."

"Thank you, Rachel; I'm glad you're enjoying it."

I would be enjoying it more, if Scott hadn't been here, Rachel thought, noting that Scott had not spoken a word since Shirley had said Grace.

Finally Shirley appeared to have had enough. "Come on you two, say something. You could cut the atmosphere with a knife."

Rachel was highly embarrassed, and at a loss for words, but Shirley made matters worse. "Scott's just put out because I used to try to match him up with nice Christian girls. I was always inviting a nice girl over for dinner when I'd invited him too. That's in the past," she added for emphasis, glaring at Scott.

Rachel looked at Scott, expecting him to be furious and sporting a bright red face, but to her surprise, he laughed. "I must admit, when I saw you here, Rachel, I thought Mom was at it again. Although I must admit, you're not the usual type she tries to set me up with."

"What is the usual type?" Rachel asked without thinking, and then silently berated herself.

"Well, there was the last one. I had to get a restraining order against her. She turned out to be a stalker."

"That was last year." Shirley's tone was aggrieved. "I haven't played matchmaker since. I thought she was a nice, Christian girl. I had no idea she had such, err, problems."

Rachel smiled. "My mother's played matchmaker for me for years."

"Without success, I take it?"

"Yes, Shirley, definitely without success, and unwanted at that." Rachel laughed.

Shirley pressed on. "So you've never been engaged or anything like that?"

"No, never. I did date some boys from our Church group on campus, but I didn't..." Rachel faltered, realizing she had said too much already in the presence of Scott Miller.

Shirley chose that precise moment to clear the plates, refusing offers of help. Rachel and Scott again sat in uncomfortable silence until Shirley returned with the German Black Forest Cherry Christmas cake.

This time, Scott broke the silence. "This is so delicious. It's the best cake I've ever tasted. Oh, no offense, Mom."

Shirley did not appear to mind. "You are such a good cook, Rachel. Your cake is wonderful; I can't wait for the recipe." She laughed and patted her ample stomach. "I have a coffee cake too, which we can have after a little break of course, to let our meal settle. Then we can have it with coffee."

Rachel groaned inwardly. She did not want the evening to stretch on any longer than possible. She did not feel she could eat two desserts, and furthermore, she wanted to get away with all haste from the unbearable, yet strangely attractive, Dr. Scott Miller.

There is no fear in love; but perfect love casteth out fear: because fear hath torment. He that feareth is not made perfect in love.
(1 John 4:18)

Chapter Six.

Rachel was unspeakably relieved when the evening came to an end. She wanted nothing better than to get back home and crawl into bed, pull the covers over her head, and wish that the evening had never happened. Unfortunately, Scott decided to leave at the same time as Rachel did. In her hurry to leave, she slipped on the ice on the sidewalk and Scott seized her arm to steady her. Little electric currents coursed through her body at his touch. He did not let go, but held her arm all the way to her car.

Rachel fought the urge to push him away.

When they reached her car, Scott pointed. Rachel followed his direction and her heart sank. A flat tire, and the rim was resting on the ground. "Oh no!"

"I'll change it for you. Go back to Mom's and wait inside, in the warmth."

"I don't have a spare."

"You don't have a spare?" Scott's tone was incredulous. He looked down at her as if she had totally lost her senses.

"No. I've been meaning to get that organized since I got here, but, well, I've just had so much on my mind," she finished lamely. "I'll just call a cab." Rachel fished in her purse for her cell phone.

"I'll give you a ride." The tone was one of command.

"No, really, I..."

Scott had Rachel by the arm again and was steering her to his white pickup. The words, "Wild Oak Animal Clinic," were emblazoned in large black print on the side of the vehicle.

No wonder he didn't believe that I'd overlooked that, Rachel thought.

"I'll call Mom later and tell her your car will be outside her house 'til tomorrow."

Rachel spoke before he could offer any further help, although she was relieved that he was giving her a ride. Waiting in the cold for a cab would be no fun at all. "My sister can take me to get another tire on my lunch break tomorrow."

Scott merely nodded, but then seemed to think the better of it. "On second thought, just do it first thing in the morning. It won't matter if you're late, just this one time."

Rachel murmured her thanks. The rest of the time taken to drive to Rachel's house was passed in silence, apart from Rachel giving Scott directions. The whole time, Rachel was aware of Scott's electric presence, which set her heart racing.

Get a grip, she told herself.

When Scott's truck pulled up, Rachel hastily muttered her thanks and wanted to get as far away from him as she could. However Scott had other plans. "It's dark. I'll walk you to the door."

"It's perfectly safe. There's no one about, only deer, pheasants, and wild turkeys."

Scott did not reply, but merely walked around and opened the door for Rachel. In her haste to get to the front door, she slipped again on the ice, and again Scott took her arm. As they approached the front door, the motion sensor light turned itself on, illuminating the whole front of the house. Rachel was blinking so hard that she did not see her sister Dinah standing in the doorway.

"Hi, Rachel, who do you have here?"

Rachel was annoyed that Dinah's voice was dripping sensuality. When her vision cleared she saw that Dinah was wearing tight jeans and a pretty, powder blue, cashmere sweater. What's more, her make up looked flawless.

Who wears make up in their own house at this time of night? Rachel thought crossly.

"Dinah, this is my boss, Dr. Scott Miller. Scott, this is my sister, Dinah."

"Please call me Scott."

Rachel was taken aback. Scott's tone was nothing short of charming. Up to this moment, she had only heard him speak in a most matter of fact voice and at times even abruptly. "I have a flat tire so Scott gave me a ride. Would you mind taking me to get another one first thing in the morning, Dinah?"

"Of course not. You know I'm always helping you out." Dinah ignored Rachel's scowl and turned back to Scott. "Would you like to come in for a hot drink? It's so cold out here."

"No, he was just on his way," Rachel began, but Scott cut her off.

"I don't mind if I do. Thank you."

What is he playing at? Rachel was annoyed. She pushed in front of Scott and walked into the house, and then over to the blazing fire. When she turned around, she saw Dinah and Scott in conversation, their heads together, and then Scott laughed. *Dinah's at her flirty best*, Rachel thought, irritated. *Just when I thought the evening was safety over - can it get any worse?*

Rachel stood at the fire and warmed her hands. Scott soon came over and sat in one of the chairs closest to the fire, while Dinah went away to put on the coffee pot. Rachel made no attempt to initiate conversation, but Scott spoke.

"It seems like there's floor heating?"

"Yes."

"Still, there's nothing like a fire. They're always so nice and comforting."

Rachel merely nodded.

Undeterred, Scott pressed on. "There must be good trails for riding around here?"

"Yes, Dad and I used to ride a lot."

At that moment Dinah returned with coffee and set down steaming mugs in front of Rachel and Scott.

"Is Mom asleep?"

"Yes, she had one of her migraines and went to bed early."

"That's no good. Poor Mom."

Dinah murmured agreement, and then turned her attention to Scott. "It's lovely to meet someone Rachel works with, Scott. I haven't met anyone she works with before. Tell me all about yourself."

"There's nothing much to tell, really."

Dinah laughed, a high, tinkling laugh. "I'm sure there's lots to tell. Are you married?"

Could she be any more obvious? Rachel thought, annoyed and a little embarrassed at Dinah's overtly flirtatious manner.

"No." Scott appeared amused.

"So you've never been married? No kids?"

Rachel thought she saw something pass across Scott's face, but again he answered evenly, "No," although this time he did not look amused.

Dinah fixed him with a bright smile. "Mom will be so sorry she missed you. Please come to dinner with us one night soon."

Oh please God, let him refuse; please God, let him refuse, Rachel chanted under her breath. She was fairly sure that he would refuse, but to her surprise and dismay he accepted the dinner invitation.

"That would be lovely, Dinah; how kind of you."

Nothing kind about it, you silly man, Rachel thought, *Dinah has her sights set on you. How can men be so dense? Oh, unless that's what he wants? He's being awfully nice to her. I haven't heard him so nice since I met him; he usually just barks out orders.*

That night, Rachel was unable to sleep for hours. She tossed and turned, apprehensive that Scott appeared to be interested in her sister, and even more so, anxious at the fact that it bothered her.

"Go to now, ye that say, Today or to morrow we will go into such a city, and continue there a year, and buy and sell, and get gain:" "Whereas ye know not what [shall be] on the morrow. For what [is] your life? It is even a vapour, that appeareth for a little time, and then vanisheth away."
(James 4:13-14)

Chapter Seven.

On the way to buy a new tire, Dinah grilled Rachel about Scott. "Does he have a girlfriend?"

"Not as far as I know."

"What were you doing out late with him last night?"

"His mother also works at the clinic. I didn't know she was his mother and we met at Church and she invited me back for dinner, and he was there too."

Dinah snorted as she pulled off the road. "I'll wait in the car for you. He still doesn't live with his mother, does he?"

"No, nothing like that. She'd invited him for dinner too."

"Was she trying to set the two of you up together?"

Rachel expelled her breath sharply. "No, nothing like that, Dinah. I'll be right back."

On the way to Rachel's car, Dinah pursued the subject. "Are you interested in Scott?"

"Of course not."

"Don't 'of course not' me, Rachel. I know you must be desperate for a boyfriend by now, and he's very attractive, don't you think?"

"Can we change the subject, Dinah? You haven't said a word about anything else all day. It's bad enough that I have to work with him; I don't want to hear about him all day too. Date him if you like, only don't tell me about it."

Dinah pulled up outside Shirley's house next to Rachel's car and eyed Rachel speculatively. "Why would you mind if I dated Scott? You know what I think? I think you're attracted to him too and you want him for yourself, only you won't admit it."

With that, Dinah left Rachel on the roadside and drove away, leaving Rachel to change the tire all by herself.

Rachel arrived at the vet clinic dirty and flustered. Could there be some truth in what Dinah had said? Is that why she didn't want Dinah and Scott to be a couple?

"Thank goodness you're here; I was about to call you." Linda, the receptionist, hurried around the desk and drew Rachel into the little room behind the office. "It's crazy today! Scott's at a fence injury at Four Corners Breeding Farm, Paul's in surgery with a dog hit by a car, Kenneth's doing an emergency caesarean on a poodle and that only leaves you, and just before you walked through the door, we had an emergency call from an elderly lady who said her mare is foaling - in the middle of winter at all times of year - and it's a bad malpresentation. You'll have to hurry, and we can't spare a nurse."

Rachel sprang into action. "Quick, give me the address."

Just then, Annette walked in the room. "You're sending Rachel to the foaling? But Scott said not to send her out of the surgery."

Linda glared at Annette, and then said, "It's an emergency, Annette."

Rachel registered what Annette had said, but knew there was no time to waste. A mare always foals quickly, and any delay can be fatal. Mares are not like cows. Many a time someone had checked a mare that showed no signs of foaling, only to check ten minutes later to find a foal already born.

Linda handed Rachel the keys to the company truck. "Everything you need's in there."

Rachel drove out quickly to the farm which thankfully was not far away. An elderly woman was waiting for her. "Quick, in here."

She led Rachel to a stall where the mare was standing up, and the foal was presenting with head and one leg. Rachel immediately hurried into the stall. "Quick, you hold the mare's head." She felt for the other leg which was pushed back at an awkward angle over the shoulder. Normally, a veterinarian would push the foal back and then correct the position, but it was too late for this. With some difficulty, Rachel finally managed to hook the leg over the shoulder and get it into position. Once that was done, she was able to deliver the foal, which was very heavy and the mare was still standing.

Rachel could not drop the foal, so tried to lower the foal to the ground gently. It took all her strength. She immediately cleared the foal's airway but the foal was breathing nicely and immediately sat up. "She's okay," she called to the elderly woman, who let go of the mare's head and came around to Rachel, and then immediately burst into tears.

Rachel, herself close to tears of relief, put her arm around the woman, and led her to the edge of the stall so the mare could inspect her new baby. The mare lost no time. She nickered in delight at the sight of the foal, then licked the baby hard, and then chewed on her ears, which made both the lady and Rachel laugh.

"I'm Jean."

"I'm Rachel. Nice to meet you, Jean."

Jean burst into flood of tears, and then managed to say, "Will they be alright?"

"I can't see why not," Rachel said. "I'll check the filly over when the mare has gotten to know her. I'll wait around and make sure she drinks okay and does all the other things on time."

"Thank you, thank you. This was my husband's favorite mare and he died eight months ago. I know it's a strange time of year for a mare to give birth, but my husband tried for years to breed this mare and this is her first ever foal. I'm not a horse person and I sold the other horses of my husband's, but he'd have a few words to say when I get to the Great Hereafter if I'd sold his favorite mare. I sold the farm and moved to this small place after he passed away." Jean peered into Rachel's face. "Aren't you Aaron Bridges' daughter?"

"Yes, that's right."

"My husband was a friend of your father's. This Quarter Horse mare is your father's bloodlines."

Rachel looked hard at the mare. "Is she one of Waldo's daughters?"

Jean nodded. Rachel had forgotten Waldo's registered name, but she and Dinah had given the prize stallion the nickname "Waldo" not long after he was born. He was unlike other foals in that he did not want to stick like glue to his mother, and always was found asleep behind a bush. Dinah and Rachel used to say for a joke, "Where's Waldo?" so the name stuck.

"I wish I had a daughter of Waldo's."

"You don't have any horses?"

"No, I had to go to college, but I do want to move to an equine practice and have horses again."

"There's nothing more lovely than a newborn foal, is there? Their soft, little velvety muzzles. The miracle of birth."

"It sure is a miracle," Rachel agreed.

"I feel bad; the foaling alarm didn't go off. I just happened to check."

"It's not your fault," Rachel reassured her. "As you know, the foaling alarm only signals when the mare lies out flat to give birth, but a mare will often stand for the beginning of labor, and also often remain standing throughout a malpresentation."

"I didn't know. I'm so shaken up after all this. Would you like a hot cocoa to warm up?"

"That would be lovely, thank you. I'll just call the clinic first to make sure I'm not wanted there." Seeing Jean's worried face, Rachel continued, "Don't worry; if I have to go back to the clinic, I'll come back here to make sure the foal is passing her milestones in the first couple hours."

Jean gushed her relief then went to make hot cocoa, while Rachel called the clinic.

"Great that the foal's okay," Linda said, "It must have been touch-and-go as far as time went. Everything's quiet now here, thank goodness."

"Call me if you need me. The client is an elderly lady and she's quite distressed. I just want to make sure the foal is on her feet and drinking well before I leave."

"That should be fine. I'll call if we need you."

Jean returned with two mugs of hot chocolate just as the filly tried to stand. Her efforts were comical, and the two women laughed. "She seems quite a big, strong filly," Rachel said.

Finally she was on her feet but looked everywhere for the milk, nuzzling the mare's knees. Jean was again concerned. "Don't worry, Jean. Sometimes foals keep doing this, and we just have to milk the mare and give the foal a bottle or two of milk, then they immediately know where and how to drink. It's amazing really. Give her more time, though."

Soon afterward, the filly got things sorted, and had a good long drink. Both Jean and Rachel were delighted and relieved. However, at that very moment, Jean said, "Someone's here."

Rachel looked up to see Scott striding into the barn. He ignored Rachel and asked Jean, "How is everything?"

"Wonderful, Scott. Rachel is a treasure. It was the worst malpresentation I'd ever seen. I'm no horse person, but I always helped my husband, and he had to deliver quite a few foals. I've never seen a malpresentation so bad. I don't know how Rachel managed, and look, the filly is doing well; she's even nursing now. I thought she would be dead, but Rachel saved her." Jean burst into tears again and Rachel put her arm around her.

"Jean, now that she's nursing well, I don't think there's any cause for concern, but how about I pop over each morning and night on my way to and from the clinic, just to check?"

"Thank you, Rachel." Turning to Scott, she said, "You've got a good horse vet there. Better hang onto her."

Rachel walked out, careful not to look at Scott's face. Just as she had her hand on the door to the company's truck, Scott walked over to her. "Well done, Rachel," he said. "Great job." He patted her on her shoulder.

A warm feeling ran through Rachel, and she smiled to herself all the way back to the vet clinic. *I'm one step closer to being an equine vet*, she thought, but then couldn't discount the fact that her happiness may have been in part for personal reasons, not solely career.

He hath made every [thing] beautiful in his time: also he hath set the world in their heart, so that no man can find out the work that God maketh from the beginning to the end. (Ecclesiastes 3:11)

Chapter Eight.

"You won't get far without these."

Rachel turned around to see Dinah standing there, looking quite smug, one hand on her hip and the other hand jangling Rachel's keys in the air.

"Oh, I thought they were in my purse." Rachel retraced her steps back into the house and took the keys from Dinah.

Rachel's mom, Carole, appeared with a mug of coffee and a plate of toast. "Here Rachel, eat this. You haven't had any breakfast."

"Sorry, mom, I'm late. I can't."

"Rachel, you can't work on an empty stomach." Rachel's mom liked to feed everyone.

"I can't be late for work. I slept through the alarm."

"Already nervous about dinner later this week, are you?" Dinah's tone was teasing.

"Why would I be?" Rachel called over her shoulder as she raced for the door. She had slept through her alarm after spending a restless night, thanks to a vivid dream of Scott and

Dinah getting married. "A nightmare more like it," she said aloud to herself as she reached her car.

Rachel reached the clinic on the stroke of nine, and encountered Scott at the front desk. "I have a horse call; would you like to come with me?"

Rachel was taken aback by Scott's unexpected offer. "What, now?"

"Yes. You're not booked in for surgery this morning, are you?"

Rachel shook her head. "Okay, that would be great."

"Do you need a nurse?" Annette's tone held a hint of desperation.

Rachel turned around and looked at Annette, who had been giving Rachel's back quite a nasty look.

"No, Annette, it won't be necessary." With that, Scott walked out the door followed by Rachel.

As they drove off, Rachel turned to Scott. She saw his hands on the wheel, tough, working hands. A tingle ran through her. Gathering herself together, she took a deep, steadying breath and asked, "What's wrong with the horse?"

"Lameness, but apart from that, no idea. A man called the clinic this morning and said his horse couldn't put its leg to the ground. He's a new client. He said he couldn't see an injury. Linda took the call. She said it was hard to get any information out of him and that he seemed very distressed. It sounds like a severe lameness."

"Laminitis." Rachel said the word as much to herself as to Scott, who merely shrugged.

"Yes, that's the most obvious, severe laminitis, but we'll know soon enough."

The rest of the time was spent in silence, an uncomfortable silence for Rachel, who wished Scott would say something, anything. Her stomach was gurgling, not too loudly, but Rachel was embarrassed and concerned that Scott could hear. She was hungry and wished she had taken the offered toast and eaten it in the car, no matter how many crumbs she would have spilled.

I really need to start thinking ahead, she scolded herself.

Scott drove down a little, tree-lined lane and pulled up next to a man and a crying girl who was holding a fat gray pony. The pony was leaning back.

"Yep," Scott said, as he climbed out of the car. Rachel knew he was referring to her guess of laminitis.

The man, who was tall, and good looking in a rugged way, introduced himself as Caleb Keener.

Scott picked up the lame foot and the pony was not happy at all. Rachel comforted the young girl. "Betsy is my pony. She's not going to die, is she?"

Rachel patted the little girl on the head then knelt down beside her.

"Betsy will need to eat special food, and no matter how much you want to, you can't give her treats any more."

"Not even carrots?" The little girl pulled on a loose strand of hair and sounded wistful.

"Especially not carrots. What's your name?"

"Audra." The little girl sniffed.

"Look, Audra, Betsy is very fat and when ponies get too fat, it hurts their feet very badly. If you feed her apples or carrots, although Betsy likes them, it hurts her feet badly and she can't walk. You don't want to cause Betsy pain, do you?"

Audra shook her head. "Is she going to be okay?"

Rachel considered what to say. "She must never again eat any treats, and she must always eat what we tell you to give her. This is very important. Can you do that? If you do that, Betsy will be okay, but if you feed her treats, she will be in a lot of pain again."

"I promise."

Rachel stood up to speak to the father, who had been listening intently, but then she turned her attention to Scott. "Will I hold Betsy while you X-ray?"

"Yes." Scott was back to monosyllables again, but Rachel didn't mind as he was treating the horse.

Rachel took Betsy from the father, and said, "Scott is taking X-Rays. Betsy has laminitis."

"Is that the same as founder?"

Rachel nodded. "Yes, same thing, different words. Betsy is IR. That means 'insulin resistant.'"

"Is that like diabetes in people?"

"Kind of. She is very overweight. See those fat pads above her eyes?"

Caleb nodded.

"And see those bulges of fat on her rump?"

Caleb nodded again. "Do I have to starve her to get her thin?"

"Not at all, that would be the worst thing you could do. She needs to keep eating, specifically eat beet pulp and hay which is low in NSCs. Oh, that means non structural carbohydrates. When I get back to the clinic, I'll write out a feeding regime for you. You need to stick to it like glue," Rachel said. "I mean it. Carrots are full of sugar and any treats could," she hesitated, "prove very bad, if you get my meaning."

Caleb looked serious. "I'll be very careful. I'll see she only gets what you say and nothing else. I'll keep a close eye on Audra. Since my divorce, this pony has become all Audra ever thinks about. We moved here two months ago, and the pasture is different here. I guess I didn't realize just how fat Betsy had gotten."

Scott had finished with the X-Rays and took the machine and the plates to his pickup, then returned with trimming gear. "Caleb, I'm going to give her anti inflammatories which also provide pain relief. I'm going to trim her hooves, and then I'm going to tape a pad to this hoof which will give her a lot of relief. Call me if she tears it off, but I'll be back to check in two days. I'll give her an injection now, and I'll give you some powders to put in her feed twice a day."

As Rachel took down Caleb's details, she said, "Give me your email address too, then I can email you a link to a very good online support group for I.R. horses. I'll also email you the feeding regime. Now, you will be very careful to change over the feed slowly, won't you, as horses can't tolerate a sudden change in feed. If you drop over to the clinic this afternoon, I'll have a probiotic ready for you too. It's helpful in laminitis, and you can just put it in her feed."

Rachel stopped speaking, as she noticed that Scott was staring intently at her. *Oh dear, I hope I haven't stepped out of line*, she thought.

[A Song of degrees for Solomon.] Except the Lord build the house, they labour in vain that build it: except the Lord keep the city, the watchman waketh [but] in vain.
(Psalm 127:1)

Chapter Nine.

Scott did not speak while they were driving down the lane, and Rachel was nervous, waiting for a reprimand. Her stomach grumbled louder than ever. Rachel cleared her throat, hoping that would disguise the noise.

"You seem to know a lot about nutrition for laminitis," Scott said when they turned out of the lane.

Rachel did not detect any note of reproach in his advice, but nevertheless remained wary. "I took Equine Nutrition classes within my degree, provided by the University Of Edinburgh."

"I didn't know that." Scott sounded genuinely surprised.

"It's on my résumé." *I'll bet he didn't even look at it,* Rachel thought, *given that he was biased against me right from the start.*

"Oh, I must have overlooked that part. You went to Scotland?"

"No, it's an online course, and I did others as well, including one specializing in nutrition for laminitis. I really think that the pony should go on jiaogulan."

Scott looked over at her, and then handed her his cell phone. "Check that for any messages from the clinic will you?"

Rachel did as he asked, then handed it back. "Nothing."

"Good, I need to hear more about jio, jia, whatever that word was. I'm ashamed to say I've never heard of it before. Now is an opportune time given the elevated G.I.T. sounds."

Rachel was puzzled, and looked at Scott. He turned to her, clearly amused, as her stomach grumbled loudly again. "Lunch?"

Rachel flushed bright red at her traitorous stomach's rumblings, but then she realized that Scott was using the veterinary term to refer to a rumbling stomach. She laughed, and most of her nervousness faded.

Scott laughed too. "We should have time for a quick bite of lunch before heading back to the clinic, and you can fill me in on..." Scott hesitated.

"Jiaogulan," Rachel supplied.

"Yes." Scott pulled into a parking lot outside a gray stone building, which looked like it, or at least the front section, may have spent its early days as a Church building.

The inside was all stone and rich mahogany wood, and the dark ambience gave it an intimate, romantic feel, much to Rachel's discomfort. *This is awkward; it feels a bit like a date,*

Rachel thought. To make matters worse, the waitress appeared to assume that Scott and Rachel were in fact a couple, and quickly seated them in a private corner. Scott did not appear to have noticed, as far as Rachel could tell.

"We'll order first, and then you can fill me in." Scott did not look up from studying the menu. "Oh, by the way, my treat, or rather, it will come out of my clinic account. Eat up. I can't have my vets fainting from hunger, especially if they're going to work on horses."

Rachel's heart skipped a beat.

Did he say what I thought he said? Work on horses?

Rachel could barely contain her excitement, but did not say a word in response. Instead, she too studied the menu, although she had all but lost her appetite in the excitement.

"I'll have the Bacon-Scallion Whipped Potatoes with Sour Cream and Balsamic Red Onion Marmalade, please," Rachel said to the waitress, who then turned and looked at Scott. Rachel noted that the waitress looked at Scott appreciatively, and she was annoyed.

That's quite rude of her, given that she obviously thinks we're a couple, Rachel thought. *She's looking him up and down, and she's speaking to him in that flirtatious voice.*

"And may I have the Rustic Flatbread and Traditional Minestrone Soup, Prosciutto with Caramelized Red Onions, please." Scott fixed the waitress with his best smile, and Rachel could not help but scowl. Scott turned his attention back to Rachel. "Now, while we're waiting for our meals, fill me in."

"Okay. Jiaogulan is a Chinese herb used in Traditional Chinese Medicine, but recent veterinary trials have been run on its use in laminitis, and there's been considerable success."

"Can you email me references to the trials?" Scott interrupted.

"Sure. In some cases it's had quite dramatic effects." Rachel stopped as Scott held up his hand.

"Now say it slowly so I'll know how to pronounce it."

"It's pronounced *jee - aw - goo -lan* as far as I know, but others may pronounce it differently."

Scott nodded and waved her on.

"It encourages good circulation in the hooves and promotes hoof growth and has an anti-clotting effect. If a horse has infection in the feet, it will make the horse more lame to start with, and any brewing abscesses will surface and drain in the first few weeks on it."

Scott looked interested. "Any contra-indications?

"Yes, you can't give it to a horse with a heart condition or a horse that's dehydrated. It can't be used at the same time as aspirins, any nonsteroidal anti-inflammatories, oh, or heparin of course." Rachel stopped to consider. "There's a whole list of things it can't be given with. I have a stack of notes at home on it; I could copy them for you if you'd like."

"Yes, thank you, I'd like that." Scott fixed Rachel with the same beaming smile he had given the waitress, and Rachel didn't know whether or not she should be pleased at that.

The meals arrived, and for a while both ate in silence, which was only interrupted when Scott asked a question at intervals about nutrition for a horse with laminitis.

At the end of the course, Scott asked, "Dessert?" after checking his cell phone.

"Yes, please." Rachel was thoroughly enjoying discussing equine veterinary matters.

The waitress returned, smiling at Scott, but took Rachel's order first.

"I think I'll have the Chocolate Vanilla Cake with Salted Caramel please. What's it like?"

"It comes with vanilla-bean ice cream and roasted peanuts," the waitress said abruptly, then turned to Scott. "And what would you like, sir?"

Oh come on, Rachel thought crossly, *she's actually batting her eyelids at him.*

Scott returned the waitress's expansive smile, much to Rachel's annoyance. "The Flourless Chocolate Mud Cake please."

"Oh it's divine," the waitress gushed. "It's made without flour. Oh silly me, it says that, doesn't it." She giggled, and ran her hand through her over processed, white-blonde hair so harshly that Rachel thought that some of it might snap off. "It's made with a dozen eggs, and it is so rich and creamy, and it's served with whipped cream. It's my favorite."

Scott merely nodded, and the waitress left, seemingly disappointed by his lack of response. Scott leaned over to Rachel. "I saw you rolling your eyes then."

Rachel did not know what to say. "Um, it's just, um, interesting, the effect you have on women."

Scott looked startled, and then said, "Jealous?" in an amused voice.

Rachel was horror-stricken and struck speechless.

How could he say such a thing?

She just sat and looked shocked, much to Scott's obvious amusement.

Am I jealous? she wondered. *Is he joking, or can he see that I'm jealous? I must be jealous.*

Rachel was in a state of agitation. She suddenly felt nauseous, so excused herself and went to the bathroom.

The bathroom was quite beautiful, all stone and tile, but Rachel was in no mood to admire it. All she wanted to do was splash water on her face, but to her frustration, the sensors on the faucets did not appear to work. Finally one worked after Rachel tapped it hard on the top of the spout.

Rachel sighed deeply as the cool water splashed on her skin. She took a deep breath and looked at her reflection in the mirror. *Am I really jealous?* she wondered.

Am I attracted to him? Well yes, but he is a good looking man, who wouldn't be attracted to him? But surely I don't have romantic ideas about him.

Rachel frantically splashed more water on her face, as if that would help her think more clearly. Alas, it did not. She returned to the table with her head in turmoil.

Scott looked up and smiled at her upon her return. "Sorry, we have to get the desserts to go. The clinic just called; we'd better be heading back."

Rachel returned his smile and nodded. She noted that the waitress beamed at Scott as she handed them their desserts.

As they pulled up at the clinic, Scott turned to Rachel. "I'm impressed with your knowledge of equine nutrition, I must say, and that you're up with the latest treatments. You know what they say, that someone straight out of vet school has the edge on all us old timers." He laughed. "Would you like to take over Caleb Keener as a client?"

Rachel was astonished. "What? You mean, all by myself?"

Scott nodded.

"You don't think Caleb will mind?"

Scott fixed her with a steely gaze. "On the contrary, I think Caleb will be delighted. Surely you saw the way he was looking at you?" With that, Scott walked back into the clinic, leaving Rachel trailing in his wake.

Surely Scott can't be jealous? she asked herself. *Oh goodness me, I really need time to think. Scott did sound jealous; surely he can't be interested in me in a romantic way? And if he is, what would I do?*

Rachel had no time to ponder the issue any further, as Annette was waiting for her at the door, hands on hips. "You were away a long time." Her tone was almost accusatory.

Rachel did not owe her an explanation by any means, so simply nodded and pushed past her.

Then said he also to him that bade him, When thou makest a dinner or a supper, call not thy friends, nor thy brethren, neither thy kinsmen, nor [thy] rich neighbours; lest they also bid thee again, and a recompence be made thee.
But when thou makest a feast, call the poor, the maimed, the lame, the blind:
And thou shalt be blessed; for they cannot recompense thee: for thou shalt be recompensed at the resurrection of the just.
(Luke 14:12-14)

Chapter Ten.

Friday came too soon for Rachel, who had wanted time for herself to think and pray, but the clinic had kept her busy. Betsy the pony was already showing signs of improvement, and Jean's foal was doing well, but Rachel had been given no other large animals to treat. Instead, the days had been full of routine treatments on small animals at the clinic. Scott had been conspicuous by his absence too, being away on farm visits all week. Rachel had noted that Annette had scheduled herself to attend with Scott most days.

Rachel did not know whether she was looking forward to the coming night, as Scott had accepted Dinah's invitation to join Dinah, Rachel, and their mother, Carole, for dinner. Rachel was still undecided as to whether she had feelings for Scott. Dinah had refused all offers of Rachel's to help with the dinner, and Rachel could not help the sinking suspicion that Dinah was up to something.

At three minutes to five, an elderly dog suspected of having a stroke was rushed in by its worried owner, and Rachel happened to be the only vet in the clinic. By the time she had the dog stabilized and handed over to the night nurse, it was almost seven. Rachel showered at the clinic and changed into fresh clothes, although only had work clothes on hand. She had already called Dinah and explained the situation, and urged her to start without her. She called Dinah again just as she left the clinic.

When Rachel finally got home, she saw people seated at the dining table, Dinah, their Mom, Scott, and a man who looked vaguely familiar. Rachel groaned inwardly, immediately becoming conscious of Dinah's plan.

She sees this as a double date, she thought, *Scott for herself, and some man she's going to try to set me up with. I really don't like blind dates at the best of times.*

Rachel was quite uneasy; not only had she not yet sorted through her feelings for Scott, but Dinah clearly wanted him for herself.

"Rachel, you're here." Dinah's greeting was enthusiastic. "I've just served, and yours is on the table, here. You know Scott, of course, but do you remember Brian?"

Rachel did not in fact remember Brian, but thought it rude to say so, so merely stared, trying to figure out how to reply. Thankfully Brian came to her rescue.

"You wouldn't have seen me since we were kids, Rachel. I went to grade school with Dinah. I've been away doing postgraduate work for years and only just came back this year. I bumped into Dinah down at the hardware store and she invited me to dinner tonight."

Rachel thought for a bit, thrown by the thought of Dinah in a hardware store, and then remembered. "Oh yes, of course, you're that Brian! You and Dinah were quite good friends at one stage. You both used to play pranks on me. Let me see." Rachel put her finger to her chin. "There was the time when you put the spider in my bed, and the time you both jumped out of the closet to scare me, and the time you cut hideous bangs in my hair when I fell asleep on the sofa one hot afternoon."

"All Dinah's fault of course."

Everyone but Scott laughed heartily, while Scott merely plastered what looked to Rachel like a fake smile on his face.

"I've seen you somewhere recently though, Brian. Your face looks familiar. Your adult face, that is," Rachel amended.

"At Church?"

"Yes! That's it. I knew I recognized you. You sit down the front with, um, with..." Rachel's voice trailed off and she tried to recall last Sunday's service.

"By myself, I expect, Rachel, sad to say." Brian's tone was one of mock sadness.

Dinah chimed in. "A good looking bachelor like you, surely not, Brian. You and Rachel have a lot in common. I'm sure you'll have lots to talk about."

Rachel glared at Dinah, and kicked her under the table.

"Ouch." Scott bent down and rubbed his leg.

Rachel's face went bright red as she realized she had kicked Scott instead of Dinah, and debated whether or not to apologize, as that would alert Brian to her actions. She decided to keep silent, and avoided Scott's eyes. Dinah had seated herself next to Scott, and opposite Rachel, and had seated Brian next to Rachel. Their mother was seated at the head of the table, and now chose this moment to speak.

"Don't you have singles groups at church, Brian? Rachel dear, you should join a singles group. You need to meet a nice man. You're not getting any younger, you know. I do want to be a grandmother. I always said it was a mistake you wanting to be a career woman. You'll look back in your old age when you're living all alone, surrounded by dogs and cats, and regret that you never married. Mark my words."

Rachel could not have been more embarrassed if she tried. She stared at her creamy chicken and wild rice soup.

"Oh, Mom, stop; you're embarrassing Rachel. She's turned a horrible shade of red. Actually, Brian, do you have a singles group at your Church?"

"Yes, as matter of fact, we do."

"You're not allowed to marry outside the Church, isn't that right?"

Brian laughed. "Oh dear, you make us sound like a cult. You must be thinking of the Scripture that says not to be unequally yoked with unbelievers."

Rachel wished the floor would literally open up and swallow her. She swirled her spoon around her soup, and kept her head down.

Dinah pressed on, undaunted. "What does that mean, exactly?"

"It means that a Christian should only marry another Christian."

"And dating, what about dating? Should a Christian only date another Christian?"

Rachel stole a glance at Brian who had turned quite solemn. "Yes. I know that sounds strange to non-Christians, but it makes sense when you think about it. A Christian dating a non-Christian is becoming more common and more accepted these days, but it does bring with it certain problems. For a start, the two people will have completely different values. One will put Christ first, above everything, and the other will not be able to understand that. If you are married to someone who doesn't love Jesus, you're just asking for all sorts of problems."

Rachel admired the way Brian spoke up, and looked at Scott, only to see he had turned white and seemed to be clenching his jaw quite hard.

"Isn't it the case that there's no intimacy before marriage too, Brian?" Dinah asked in a saccharine tone.

I know she has an agenda with all this, Rachel thought darkly.

Brian looked a little embarrassed, but answered readily enough. "Yes, that's right."

Carole piped up, "I read about The Silver Ring Thing some years back."

"What was that about, Mom?"

Brian answered Dinah. "The Silver Ring Thing was a program that encouraged people to remain celibate until marriage, and promoted rings along with a vow. You know, the chastity rings, the promise rings."

"Oh, yes, I've heard of those," Dinah said while shooting Rachel a glance under her eyelashes. "Do you think that's a good idea, Rachel?"

"Yes, certainly." Rachel wondered where Dinah was going with all this.

"Rachel's been a good Christian and a Churchgoer as long as I can remember," Dinah continued. "Dad was a Christian too."

"What about you, Dinah? Do you have faith?"

Rachel admired Brian for coming straight out and asking.

Dinah's response was a hollow, false laugh. "Oh Brian, you want to get me to come to Church?" With that, she started to clear the table, refusing all offers of help.

"Dinah, you should come along one day. Rachel and I would be glad to have you."

Dinah left the room with haste, and Rachel noted that Scott was clearly uncomfortable and shifting in his seat.

Perhaps he's afraid that Brian will invite him to Church next, she thought. *Now I have one more problem to think about. I thought Scott was a Christian, even though he doesn't go to Church. If he isn't a Christian, then I can't really date him. Oh, but do I even want to? What am I going to do? I have tomorrow off; I need to seek the Lord on this and get my head straight.*

Dinah returned with the stuffed pork loin. There was, for a time, a respite in the conversation, although Dinah did make small talk at intervals, and continually touched Scott's arm in a possessive way when she did so.

Rachel did not know what to think. Clearly Dinah had designs on Scott, and also wanted to set her up with Brian. However, while Brian was nice, and a Christian as well, there was simply no spark whatsoever. Rachel was not attracted to him.

Scott, who had been looking increasingly uncomfortable, excused himself before dessert, much to Rachel's disappointment. Dinah and Carole went to the kitchen, clearly to leave Brian and Rachel alone.

Both Rachel and Brian sat in uncomfortable silence. Finally, Brian said, "This looks like an attempt at matchmaking, I'm afraid."

Rachel laughed. "Clearly. I'm sorry; I had no idea."

Brian laughed too. "Me either. I take it you're not dating Scott? Dinah seems keen on him."

"No, I'm not dating Scott and yes, Dinah does seem keen on him." Rachel wondered whether Brian was actually attracted to Dinah, but given his stand on dating non-Christians, she doubted that was so.

> *Ointment and perfume rejoice the heart: so [doth] the sweetness of a man's friend by hearty counsel.*
> *Thine own friend, and thy father's friend, forsake not; neither go into thy brother's house in the day of thy calamity: [for] better [is] a neighbour [that is] near than a brother far off.*
> *(Proverbs 27:9-10)*

Chapter Eleven.

Rachel spent a sleepless night and following day trying to sort out her feelings for Scott, to no avail. By the time Monday came, she was no closer to the answer. "So much for a weekend off," she said aloud to herself as she pulled her little blue Lexus into the parking lot at the clinic.

It hadn't helped that Dinah had given her no peace, extolling the virtues of Brian the entire weekend, which Rachel figured was an attempt to matchmake. "They say a woman shouldn't let it bother her if she's not instantly attracted to a man," Dinah had said. "Women are never attracted to a man immediately; it always takes us a while to warm up. It's important to have a lot in common."

Is that true? Rachel wondered, recalling the conversation. *Are women never attracted to a man immediately? I was attracted to Scott immediately, though. And I've often heard of people falling in love at first sight, so I don't think Dinah can be right, not in all cases, anyway. Besides, she probably wants me out of the way to leave her way clear for Scott.*

Ever since Scott had turned the primary care of Betsy the pony over to Rachel only the week before, Scott's and Rachel's dealings with each other had become easy and tension free, and Rachel had thought that a friendship had been forming. Today, however, Scott was behaving differently. He barely greeted Rachel when she arrived at the clinic, and would not look her in the eye.

Rachel was scheduled to attend a routine horse farm visit with Scott that day, but Annette informed her, a little too cheerfully, that Kenneth was accompanying Scott instead and that Rachel had been scheduled back on routine patients at the clinic all day.

What on earth's going on with Scott? Rachel wondered.

She had wondered if something had happened to offend him last Friday night, when he left dinner early, and now that suspicion seemed to be confirmed.

Sometimes I just wish I'd never come back, Rachel thought, *it's not shaping up to be a good Christmas.*

The morning passed quickly; a Pomeranian with ear mites, a Cocker Spaniel with a broken leg, a neglected Persian cat which needed clipping (and his owner who needed a lecture, and got one), a Standard Poodle with bad breath, a cat which had been in a cat fight and needed antibiotics, four chickens with coccidiosis, and the other patients were a blur. By the time lunch time came around, Rachel hadn't even had time for a coffee.

"Rachel, lunch break," a voice boomed, and then Shirley put her head around the door. "Rachel, you've been on all morning. Come and have some lunch. You can't work right though."

Rachel obediently followed Shirley into the staff room, and took a seat at the big, polished, oak table. Shirley put a coffee down in front of her. "I got this from the new café down the road. It's one of those fancy coffees, a white chocolate hazelnut latté or some such thing. I hope you like it. I know you young people like your coffee fancy. Anyway, I figured you'd need the sugar."

Rachel was delighted. "Thanks, Shirley, that's very thoughtful of you."

Shirley sat down opposite Rachel. "Sorry I missed you at Church yesterday. I was out of town, visiting a friend who's been unwell. I got back late last night." Shirley yawned widely, and stretched. "How was your weekend?" She gave Rachel a long, searching look.

Oh dear, what do I say? Rachel wondered. *Does Shirley know that Scott came over for dinner on Friday night? If she does, I can't avoid mentioning it.*

Decided, Rachel answered. "It was fairly uneventful, except that Scott came over for dinner with Mom and my sister Dinah last Friday night."

Shirley took a sip of coffee, and then asked, "How did it go?"

"Good, thanks." When Shirley didn't respond, Rachel felt she should say more, so added, "Dinah had a friend there, Brian, a man she'd gone to school with."

"Would this be Brian from Church?"

"Yes. Do you know him?"

"Yes, he's a lovely man. Are he and Dinah dating?"

"No, not at all. I think Dinah, um...." Rachel faltered and did not finish her sentence.

"Dinah was trying to play matchmaker for you and Brian?"

Rachel laughed. "Yes."

Shirley laughed too. "And how did that go?"

"It didn't. I'm not at all interested in Brian and I can tell he feels exactly the same about me."

Shirley looked thoughtful. "Are you sure?"

"Yes, why?"

Shirley did not answer, but instead looked out the window and appeared to be studying the cars in the parking lot. Rachel felt she did not know her well enough to press the issue, so walked over and looked in the refrigerator for her sandwich.

When she returned to the table, she saw that Shirley was looking at her speculatively. "I hope you don't mind me asking, but your mother and sister don't come to Church. Do they go to another Church, or, um, are they not Christians?"

"They're not Christians," Rachel said without ado.

"Do forgive me for intruding. I know it's rude to ask. It's just that, well..." Shirley's voice trailed away and she looked most uncomfortable.

Rachel decided she might as well ask Shirley straight out. "Shirley, I know this is rude of me too to come straight out and ask, but the questions you've been asking about dinner the other night, well, it's just that you must have a reason for asking, and I would really love to know what that is."

Shirley took a deep sigh then put her head in her hands. "Scott came over at the weekend as I needed his help moving furniture around, and some help in the garden, and he was acting awfully funny. I haven't seen him act that way since, well, not for ages anyway. He was fine before dinner that night, so I figured something must have happened to upset him."

Rachel put down her sandwich and tried hard to swallow her mouthful quickly. "I know; I noticed it too. He's been weird to me all day and won't meet my eye."

Shirley nodded her agreement. "So he was fine at dinner?"

Rachel thought. "Well, he did excuse himself before dessert, and I did notice he'd turned a funny shade of green when the subject turned to God."

"That explains it." Shirley muttered something to herself then continued. "I shouldn't really tell you, as it's Scott's story to tell, but I've said too much as it is."

Rachel held her breath, wondering what Shirley was about to say.

Shirley crossed to the door, and shut it, before leaning across the table to Rachel and speaking in hushed tones. "This must go no further."

Rachel nodded.

"Scott was a good Christian, and he was engaged to a girl who went to our Church. She was also a vet but worked in a different clinic than Scott. Two months before the wedding, she broke the engagement as she'd gotten involved with a married man, who divorced his wife for her, and as far as I know, the two of them are still together."

Rachel was shocked, but Shirley continued, "To make matters worse, the man she ran away with was an assistant Youth Pastor at our Church."

Rachel gasped, but then said, "No one is immune from sin; all have sinned and fallen short of the glory of God."

"That's as it may be," Shirley said, "but Scott had a crisis of faith, and fell away from the Lord. Ever since then, he gets quite uptight if anyone mentions God to him, and he's especially upset each Christmas."

"For the word of God [is] quick, and powerful, and sharper than any twoedged sword, piercing even to the dividing asunder of soul and marrow, and [is] a discerner of the thoughts and intents of the heart."
(Hebrews 4:12)

Chapter Twelve.

Rachel was wondering where Scott was with God right now. She could see why he had been so upset, given the circumstances. Still, that hardly explained his strange behavior at dinner.

That afternoon, Rachel stayed back late after everyone else had gone home for the day. She wanted some alone time to read her Bible. Typically the only alone time she had at her mother's house was late at night, and by then she was always too tired to read, or to do anything other than fall asleep as soon as her head hit the pillow.

Rachel sat at the table in the staff room and opened her Bible. She wasn't generally someone who would read her Bible just where it fell open, but this time it opened at Second Samuel, chapter seven, and Rachel thought she'd read the passage anyway. Rachel read verses twenty eight and twenty nine aloud, "And now, O Lord God, thou art that God, and thy words be true, and thou hast promised this goodness unto thy servant: Therefore now let it please thee to bless the house of thy servant, that it may continue for ever before thee: for thou, O Lord God, hast spoken it: and with thy blessing let the house of thy servant be blessed for ever."

At that moment, the door opened, and Scott poked his head in. "Who were you talking to?"

"Myself," Rachel said, and then amended, "I was reading aloud from the Bible. You gave me quite a fright; I thought everyone had left for the day."

"Who died?" Scott did not respond to Rachel's comments, but walked over to the table.

"Excuse me?" Rachel had no idea what he was talking about.

"Don't people get closer to God when they think they're about to die, like in a plane crash, or when someone else has died?"

Rachel thought for moment. "No, I don't think that's true. Not for Christians, anyway."

O God, please help me find the right words to say to him, was the silent prayer she offered up.

"Do you think I'm reading the Bible as I must be having some sort of crisis? No, I love God's word. Just think of it, it's words for us from the Creator of everything. I always find that exciting. I take strength from reading the Bible. I like to read it as much as I can."

Scott sat down, which Rachel took as a good sign. "Does Brian hold the same views?"

"Brian? I don't know. I suppose most Christians have this view."

Scott rubbed his chin. "Your sister Dinah - is she dating Brian?"

That's a strange thing to ask, Rachel thought.

Aloud she said, "No. They're just friends; they've been friends for years."

Scott stood up, and walked over and leaned on the bench top next to the microwave. "You and Mom have become quite close, haven't you." It was a statement rather than a question.

Rachel nodded, wondering where this was going.

"Has she told you anything about me?"

Rachel did not know how to respond. She did not want to betray Shirley's confidence, but she did not want to lie either. She felt a slow red flush cover her face, starting at her neck and moving upwards.

"I can see from your reaction that the answer is 'Yes,'" Scott said. He shifted his weight from one foot to the other.

Rachel could not meet his eye. She felt strangely guilty, although she of course had done nothing wrong.

Scott continued. "I was engaged, and very much in love. I was very happy that God had blessed me with such a wonderful woman. This will sound silly and romantic for a man, but it was just as if I was living in a fairytale. Just before Christmas, she ran off with another man. Some Christmas gift for me that turned out to be! I couldn't figure out why God had let that happen. I'd always been a good Christian; I went to Church every Sunday; I gave to charity; I hadn't wronged anyone. I felt betrayed." Scott snorted. "That's an understatement, actually."

Rachel's stomach muscles clenched. *Why is he telling me all this? Why is he opening up to me? What should I say? He sounds so bitter.*

"Did you ever speak to a Pastor about it?"

Scott snorted again. "Yes, and he said to trust God and hang in there."

Rachel shifted in her seat. "That sounds like good advice."

The scowl on Scott's face showed her that he did not agree. "Anyway, I apologize. I really have no idea why I told you all this. I don't know what came over me."

"That's fine, really." Rachel was also surprised that Scott had opened up to her. "Feel free to talk any time you like."

Oh dear, that sounded so lame, she thought.

"Look, I have no idea why bad things happen to good people." She opened her Bible to the First Book of Corinthians, and read from chapter thirteen, verse twelve, "For now we see through a glass, darkly; but then face to face: now I know in part; but then shall I know even as also I am known."

Rachel looked up at Scott. "I've always taken that verse to mean that we don't know it all now, but we will when we get to Heaven. All our questions will be answered then."

"That's all fine, really, but it doesn't help at the time when you're going through something bad."

Rachel looked down at the table. "I suppose not." She looked back up at Scott. "But we have our faith in God, and we need to trust in Him at all times, and trust that He will work things out for us."

To her surprise, Scott's face lit up. "You know, you're right. I will admit that my faith was badly shaken, but I have started praying again lately, ever since..." Scott stopped speaking and left it there. He looked decidedly uncomfortable.

Rachel was surprised by his answer, as she had not thought he would have listened to her words. She thought she would push the matter a little further. "You know, Scott, you're welcome to come to Church at any time. It's a really friendly Church, and Shirley enjoys it there. You're welcome to come with us one Sunday, if you like."

"You know, I might do just that." Scott looked thoughtful, and then abruptly left the room without saying goodbye.

From her chair, Rachel watched out the staff room window as he walked to his Dodge Ram truck, and then watched as the vehicle left her line of vision through a flurry of snow.

Rachel spent the rest of the night desperately trying to come to terms with her feelings for Scott. Unable to sleep, she decided to pray. After a few minutes of prayer, Rachel realized that she was afraid.

What exactly I am afraid of? she asked herself. *Rejection? That must be it; I don't think I'm afraid of commitment. I've been so career-focused for too many years, throwing myself into my work. At times I've been too busy for God, and haven't prayed or read my Bible. I think I fell in love with Scott the first time I saw him, if I'm being completely honest with myself. I can't understand why I've struggled with my feelings for so long.*

Rachel opened her Concordance and searched the word "fear," then turned to the First Book of John, chapter four, verse eighteen, and read the verse aloud in a quiet voice, "There is no fear in love; but perfect love casteth out fear: because fear hath torment. He that feareth is not made perfect in love."

"Well that settles things," she said to herself, also aloud, as she shut her Bible and snuggled under her blankets. "I only hope Scott feels the same. I'll put my trust in God to bring me a good outcome, no matter what it happens to be."

With that, Rachel felt asleep, surrounded by the peace of God which passes all understanding.

*Fear thou not; for I [am] with thee: be not dismayed; for I [am] thy God: I
will strengthen thee; yea, I will help thee; yea, I will uphold thee with
the right hand of my righteousness.
(Isaiah 41:10)*

Chapter Thirteen.

After a good night's sleep following her prayer the night before, Rachel was quite refreshed when she arrived at the clinic.

Scott looked up from the phone. "Rachel, that was a large Thoroughbred breeding farm. One of their six-month-old colts has symptoms which make me suspect rattles, given that it's occurred on their farm previously."

"Rattlesnake, did you say?" Cindy asked. She was not a large animal nurse.

"No, I said rattles," Scott explained. "It's the layman's term for *Rhodococcus equi*. It got its name from the cough that can sound like a rattle, though usually by the time they get the cough, they've had the condition for a while. It generally shows up around the age of two months, but usually in foals that have had some sort of setback." He turned to Rachel. "Rachel, would you like to come with me?"

"Oh yes, please. I've never seen rattles before."

"This will be the first time that I've used the new scanner, too. Seems I bought it in the nick of time."

Rachel was pleased to see that Scott had lapsed into his amiable personality that he had shown her before the dinner the other night.

As the two of them drove away, Scott briefly looked over at Rachel. "Do you know the treatment for rattles?"

Sounds like he's testing me, Rachel thought.

"Yes, erythromycin and rifampin, given orally four times day and night."

"Good, and you know the dangers of that treatment?"

He is testing me! At first Rachel didn't know whether or not to be offended. *Well, he is the Head Vet*, she decided, *so he has every right to test me.*

"Yes, heat. This is a good time of year to give the treatment, as it can cause the temperature to escalate."

Scott went to speak, but Rachel cut him off. "And you're about to ask what to do in case the temperature does escalate, aren't you?"

Scott laughed. "Sorry."

"No, that's fine. The temperature should be taken every four hours, or even more often, and if it is too high, the foal can be washed down with denatured alcohol in water, which will get the temperature down quickly, or even sprayed with denatured alcohol in water from a spray bottle. In summer, of course, the mare and foal should be kept in a shady place and as cool as possible."

Scott did not reply for a moment, and Rachel was afraid she had made a mistake. When he still did not speak, she asked, "Did I get anything wrong?"

"No, not at all; textbook answer, full marks."

Rachel laughed.

"Rachel, is there anything waiting for you back in Florida? Are you happy where you're currently working? Oh, I don't mean here over Christmas; I mean your usual job in Florida."

"I do like my work there and the people I work with, but I am looking for work as an equine veterinarian."

"I've discussed with this Liam, and his wife wants him to retire. I think he's coming around to the idea, and he mentioned finding him a permanent replacement. I'd like you to consider working here permanently, as an equine vet. Liam's all in favor of it; he has every confidence in you. I must say, although I was skeptical when you first arrived, I can see you are shaping up to be a fine equine vet."

Rachel could not believe her ears. *Thank you, God*, she silently prayed. "Scott, that would be wonderful," she gushed. "Yes, I would be thrilled to work for you permanently."

Scott held up his hand. "Take some time to think it over. Don't give me your decision until after Christmas."

Rachel agreed. She could barely sit still on the rest of the way to the farm, so thrilled she was to be offered the position. This was a dream come true. All her life she had wanted to be a horse doctor, but the way had not been easy for her. This was the job of a lifetime. She could barely conceal her excitement. What's more, it was working with Scott. *The job of my dreams with the man of my dreams*, she thought. *Would could be more perfect?*

The farm was breathtakingly beautiful. They passed acres and acres of manicured pastures, with impeccable four rail, PVC, white fenced paddocks. Rachel all but gasped as they drove past the owner's residence, which for all intents and purposes could only be described as a mansion, complete with extensive gardens and security gates.

Scott pulled up in a parking lot outside a magnificent carriage house which had clearly been converted to an office, given the large sign which hung above the entrance. Even the snow could not disguise the fact that the landscaping here was likewise impressive, and extended to the stallion barn, complete with water feature at the entrance. The interior of the office was just as imposing. Plush leather armchairs welcomed them, and timber features surrounded them. Rachel noted that there was even a media room.

Scott was directed to the broodmare barn, so Scott and Rachel went back to the car. The broodmare barn was a considerable drive, as far as farms go, from the main office. To Rachel's surprise, this section of the farm did not show the same evidence of immaculate upkeep as the public spaces she had just seen.

Scott pulled into a small parking lot and Rachel surveyed the area. There was a small barn, and the fencing here was wood, and well overdue for a fresh coat of paint. "The public doesn't come as far as this," Scott said under his breath to Rachel.

A man was standing outside the barn, arms crossed and leaning on the wall. He oozed an unmistakable air of boredom.

Scott introduced Rachel to the man who turned out to be the stable foreman, and the foreman, from that time on, kept giving Rachel sidelong glances of admiration.

Scott set up the scanner, and the foreman held the colt just in front of his anxious mother. "See these abscesses here, Rachel?"

Rachel studied the screen and looked carefully at the abscesses on the colt's lungs.

Scott addressed the foreman, "It's rattles all right, but not a bad case as far as rattles goes. The abscesses are quite small. You know the treatment; we've been through this before. Next time, though, I'd like you to call me as soon as you see any signs of ill thrift. This colt is small for his age, and not carrying enough weight. Now, remember to have someone take his temperature frequently."

"Yes, I'm on top of it," the foreman said, smiling at Rachel.

Scott continued. "As you do have rattles in the soil on this farm, try not to have anyone kicking up any dust when they drive past the broodmare fields. Also, don't overcrowd the pastures, like I said last time."

The foreman seemed offended. "They're all well fed!" His tone was indignant.

"I'm talking about the dust in the pastures. It's dust that's the problem with rattles. I also suggest you make an appointment with Rachel to look at your nutrition, as that does play an important part."

The foreman beamed at Rachel. "Sure, I'll do that. For sure," he repeated, still smiling widely, showing a full set of teeth.

If he was a horse I would be able to tell his age from a distance, Rachel thought.

"And next time, call me earlier." Scott's tone was harsh. Scott gave the man a tube and a container of the two antibiotics, and repeated the instructions. "He may only need one course, but keep in touch in case he needs another course."

The foreman kept smiling and nodding at Rachel.

Scott packed the scanner into his truck, and then he and Rachel drove away. "At least we know that he'll make an appointment soon for you to straighten out their nutrition." Scott laughed a dry, almost bitter laugh.

"Yes, nutrition is very important. I noticed some of their mares were a little too thin."

"True, but I meant that you made quite an impression on the foreman. I don't suppose he's ever seen a vet as attractive or you - or a woman for that matter," Scott added as an afterthought.

Rachel was struck speechless. She was unused to compliments and did not know how to respond. However, Scott kept talking.

"A lot of those big breeding farms don't treat their horses right. Many of them do, of course, but with some, it's based on economics rather than horse welfare. The place we just visited is better than most, in that some of the farms around here will not treat a horse for rattles, given that the treatment is so expensive. They just wait to see if the foal recovers by itself."

Rachel was aghast. "That's terrible!"

"Unfortunately, you see a lot of this sort of thing as an equine vet. I actually donate my services to the rescue organizations in this area. It's quite awful to see what some people do to animals, how badly they're neglected. Does it turn you off being a horse vet?"

Rachel thought for a moment. "No, it doesn't. It's heartbreaking for sure, but if I can do good here and there, well, that's all I can hope for. One horse at a time."

The rest of the drive back to the clinic was passed in silence, and Rachel thought over the morning's events. Was Scott jealous of the foreman? It seemed so to Rachel as she replayed the scene over and over in her head.

He thinks I'm attractive, Rachel thought, her stomach entirely knotted up with happiness.

The Spirit of the Lord [is] upon me, because he hath anointed me to preach the gospel to the poor; he hath sent me to heal the brokenhearted, to preach deliverance to the captives, and recovering of sight to the blind, to set at liberty them that are bruised,
To preach the acceptable year of the Lord.
(Luke 4:18-19)

Chapter Fourteen.

By the weekend, Rachel was tired but happy. She was never scheduled on call at weekends, and woke up on Saturday morning looking forward to a relaxing weekend, her mother and sister permitting.

Even Dinah was up earlier than usual on this crisp winter morning, bubbling with excitement at setting up the Christmas tree. "You will help, won't you, Rachel?"

"Of course." Rachel laughed at Dinah's child-like enthusiasm. "I can have coffee first, can't I?"

Dinah at once poured Rachel a coffee, to the disapproval of Carole their mother.

"Rachel, you have to start eating a proper breakfast. What would you like, eggs? I'll make you some. You can't live on coffee alone. You're so thin; no wonder you haven't caught a man yet."

Rachel sighed. There really was no way to respond to such remarks. Instead, she focused on sipping coffee, trying to block out her mother lecturing her at length that her biological clock was ticking.

"And one day you'll look back, and all you'll have are your animals," her mother continued, "and you'll be sorry that all you ever cared about was your career, and that you never got married and had children. You mark my words! You wait and see!"

Rachel was saved by her cell phone. Her first thought was that it must be a clinic emergency, but as she reached for the phone she saw that the caller I.D. was Shirley.

Shirley's voice was animated. "Rachel, you'll never guess what's just happened."

Rachel waited for Shirley to continue, but when she did not, asked, "What's happened?"

"You'll never guess."

Rachel sighed. She disliked guessing games. "No, I can't guess; why don't you tell me?"

"Do you remember the heavy brocade curtains in my dining room?"

Rachel tried to recollect. "Oh yes, the red and gold regency patterned ones?"

Where could this line of conversation be going? she wondered.

"That's right. Well, Scott was over early this morning to take them down and take them to be dry cleaned for me. And you'll never guess what he said!"

Here we go again.

"No, I can't guess. What did he say?"

"He said he was coming to Church tomorrow!" Shirley's voice ended on a note of triumph.

"What? Church! You said Scott's coming to Church tomorrow? Are you serious?" Rachel was flabbergasted. She knew it must be true, as she knew Shirley would not play such a joke on her, but she could not believe her ears.

"Yes, you can imagine how shocked I was. I nearly fell over!"

Rachel laughed. "I nearly fell off my chair. Well all praise to God! I never thought I'd see the day."

"O ye of little faith," Shirley giggled. "It *is* what I've been praying for, for ages."

"I can't believe it; Scott's coming to church tomorrow," Rachel said, half to Shirley and half to herself.

In fact, Rachel was so overjoyed by the news, that she ate a large pile of fried eggs with freshly baked biscuits and gravy, to her mother's delight, but she refused the bacon.

After breakfast, Rachel and Dinah set up the Christmas tree together. Dinah was unusually quiet. "Dinah, are you all right? You seem preoccupied."

"What? Oh yes, I suppose. I wanted to ask you something, and I didn't know how."

Rachel handed up Dinah a crystal snowflake. "Just go ahead and ask."

This is a morning for mysteries, Rachel thought.

"I wanted to ask if I could go to Church with you tomorrow." Dinah looked embarrassed.

"What? You? Church?" Rachel blurted out, and then was immediately sorry for her words.

Dinah looked downcast. "What, am I such a heathen you can't imagine me going to Church?"

"No, no, nothing like that," Rachel stammered, feeling horribly remorseful. "I just had no idea you were interested."

"Well you do now." Dinah was abrupt.

I deserved that, Rachel thought.

"That would be great, Dinah; I'm excited that you want to come."

As Rachel sorted through the shining, brightly colored globes, gold angels, and etched glass ornaments, she wondered about Dinah's motives. The fact that Dinah only wanted to go to Church after she found out that Scott was going too, worried Rachel.

Perhaps she's secretly in love with Scott, Rachel thought. *That will make things really awkward. It would be wonderful if she was genuine, but she's always said catty things to me whenever I've mentioned Church.*

By Sunday morning, Dinah seemed to have second thoughts, but that passed after some persuading by Rachel. It didn't help that Carole their mom was surprised that Dinah was going to Church, and complained about being left home alone.

Rachel arrived early, hoping to settle in Dinah at Church before the crowds arrived. Shirley and Scott were there too. Shirley's face registered unmistakable surprise when she saw Dinah.

Oh no, I should have warned her, Rachel thought, after she introduced the two of them to each other.

Rachel had previously mentioned Dinah to Shirley, and had told her how Dinah had absolutely no interest in the things of God, and was very much against any Christian conversation in the house.

Shirley walked ahead between the rows of wood pews to take her seat, and Scott followed her. Rachel went to walk on next, but Dinah pushed in front of her, and so Rachel was left sitting next to Dinah, with Scott on the other side of Dinah. Rachel was quite irritated and put-out, as she feared that her suspicions about Dinah only attending Church to be near Scott were confirmed.

At that moment, Brian walked down the aisle, and asked if he could sit next to Rachel. He leaned across to greet Dinah and Scott, and Scott introduced him to Shirley. Rachel noted that Scott seemed annoyed, but she had no idea why.

Perhaps he's having second thoughts about coming to Church, she wondered.

Brian leaned over to Rachel and whispered in her ear, "Isn't it fantastic that Dinah's here."

Rachel agreed, and stole a glance at Dinah, who was already deep in conversation with Scott. Scott looked up and caught her eye, a steely expression on his face.

Oh well, the main thing is that they're both in Church, Rachel thought, but at the same time could not ignore the sinking feeling in her stomach.

Rachel sent up a silent prayer that the sermon would minister to both Scott and Dinah. She was particularly concerned as she'd had some bad experiences with taking new people to her old Church. She had finally managed to persuade her neighbor to attend, and the sermon happened to be a hellfire and brimstone sermon by a visiting Pastor who loudly declared that if someone wasn't of God then they were of the devil, all the while pointing to Rachel's neighbor. The neighbor not only did not come back to Church, she crossed to the other side of the street every time she saw Rachel.

Another time Rachel had persuaded a college friend to come with her to a student fellowship on campus, and that particular day, the minister had said that if everyone present was not prepared to give ten percent of their income to the church, then they should get up right now and leave. Rachel's friend left.

It was with great relief, then, that Rachel heard the Pastor announce that he was preaching on the Christmas story. "I am reading from First Corinthians chapter two, verse two, but don't turn there in your Bibles, as I will be preaching from Matthew. But in Second Corinthians, Paul says, 'For I determined not to know any thing among you, save Jesus Christ, and him crucified.'"

The Pastor continued, "Christmas is almost upon us, and as they say, 'Jesus is the reason for the season.' So many times we preach on aspects of Christian life, and so on, but today I am going to talk about what Jesus has done for us, how He died, and rose again on the third day, and, as the Bible says in Acts, chapter four, verse twelve, 'Neither is there salvation in any other: for there is none other name under heaven given among men, whereby we must be saved.'"

The word "amen" went up from the congregation as one, and the Pastor preached a rousing sermon on salvation, starting with Jesus' birth and finishing with Acts chapter sixteen. The Pastor told the story of how Paul and Silas had been preaching, and because of this were beaten and then thrown into prison, how Paul and Silas sang hymns, and that after that there was an earthquake, and the prison doors were thrown open. The jailer thought Paul and Silas had escaped, and drew his sword to kill himself, but Paul called out to tell him that they were still there. The jailer threw himself down in front of Paul and Silas, and said, "Sirs, what must I do to be saved?"

"And how did they answer him?" the Pastor asked. "They said, 'Believe on the Lord Jesus Christ, and thou shalt be saved.' Romans chapter ten, verse nine, says, 'That if thou wilt confess with thy mouth the Lord Jesus, and shalt believe in thine heart that God hath raised him from the dead, thou shalt be saved.' Is there anyone here today who believes in their heart that God has raised Jesus from the dead? Is anyone here who wants to confess the Lord Jesus as their personal Lord and Savior? Everyone, bow your heads and pray. I ask anyone here who wants to come out the front while we say the

Sinner's Prayer with you, or wants to recommit their life to Jesus, come forward. No one can see you; everyone has their eyes shut. Come forward, come forward." The Pastor signaled to the choir who stated singing the hymn, "Softly and tenderly Jesus is calling:

'Softly and tenderly Jesus is calling,
Calling for you and for me.
Patiently Jesus is waiting and watching,
Watching for you and for me.

Come home, come home!
Ye who are weary, come home!
Earnestly, tenderly, Jesus is calling,
Calling, O sinner, come home!

Why should we tarry when Jesus is pleading,
Pleading for you and for me.
Why should we linger and heed not His mercies,
Mercies for you and for me.

Time is now fleeting, the moments are passing,
Passing from you and from me.
Shadows are gathering, death-beds are coming,
Coming for you and for me.

Oh, for the wonderful love He has promised,
Promised for you and for me.
Though we have sinned, He has mercy and pardon,

Pardon for you and for me.'

Rachel peeked and saw a few people going out the front, then to her enormous surprise and delight, Dinah pushed past her knees, tears in her eyes.

"Do you want me to go with you?" Rachel whispered.

"Yes, please." Dinah reached for Rachel's hand.

Rachel was even more surprised and delighted when Scott followed them down the aisle.

"Repeat these words after me," the Pastor said, "but bear in mind, you have to believe. If you don't believe, saying the words means nothing. Repeat after me, 'Dear God, heavenly Father, in Jesus' name, I repent of my sins and ask for your forgiveness. I believe that your only begotten Son Jesus Christ died for me and shed His precious blood on the cross at Calvary and that God raised Him from the dead. I confess Jesus as the Lord of my life. I accept Jesus Christ as my own personal Lord and Savior. Amen.'"

The ministry team then walked down, praying with each and every person. The choir was now singing, "How Great Thou Art."

A man prayed first with Scott, then with Dinah, and then started to pray a blessing on them as a couple. "We're not a couple, just friends," Dinah said hurriedly, and the man apologized profusely, and then moved onto the next person.

Rachel noted that Scott and Dinah were holding hands, and despite being elated that Scott had recommitted his life to Christ and that Dinah had just prayed the Prayer of Salvation, Rachel was deeply upset.

*The LORD bless thee, and keep thee: The LORD make his face shine upon thee,
and be gracious unto thee: The LORD lift up his countenance upon thee, and give thee peace.*
(Num 6:24 -26)

Chapter Fifteen.

Shirley invited everyone home for lunch. "Mind you, this is spur of the moment to celebrate Scott and Dinah," she warned. "It will just be sandwiches and anything else I can find at the back of the refrigerator."

Rachel was a little distracted as Scott and Dinah spent much of the time talking closely, their heads bent together. Rachel hoped that this was because they had just shared a deep spiritual experience, Scott recommitting his life to Jesus, and Dinah a brand new Christian. Rachel continually silently berated herself for even giving any consideration at all to her feelings for Scott, given the circumstances.

With Scott and Dinah talking in a corner of the living room, Brian, Shirley, and Rachel were left to make conversation between themselves. Brian and Rachel decided to help Shirley make the sandwiches.

"Here, Rachel, could you slice the tomatoes please? Brian, could you please look for the honey glazed ham? It's in there somewhere." Shirley opened the refrigerator door and waved her hand at the contents. "Now, where's that cream cheese? I thought I'd just put it down, but it's not where I thought it was."

"It's good of you to have us all over for lunch, Shirley."

"Not at all, Rachel. I'm very excited about Scott. I've prayed for longer than I can remember that he'd come back to the Lord."

Rachel nodded. "I've prayed for Dinah and Mom for ages too. I was so shocked when Dinah said that she wanted to come to church. Isn't it funny, you pray for something for ages, and then you're shocked when it happens. So much for my faith."

Brian laughed. "You know, I've been praying for Dinah too."

"You have, Brian?" Rachel looked up from the tomatoes at Brian. "That's awfully good of you."

Brian flushed red, and then turned to Shirley. "Here's the ham; now what can I do next?"

"Did you happen to see any sliced, smoked turkey in there?"

"I think I did." Brian retrieved the turkey, and set it on the bench top. "Scott and Dinah seem deep in discussion."

Shirley and Rachel's eyes met, and then Shirley looked away quickly. "Understandable, really. They're probably comparing experiences."

Shirley doesn't sound convinced, Rachel thought. *It seems the three of us are all thinking the same thing. I must have been crazy to think Scott was attracted to me; it's obvious he wants Dinah.*

Shirley, Rachel, and Brian took the sandwiches into the dining room, passing Scott and Dinah on the way.

"I'm so sorry; how rude of us not to help," Dinah said.

Rachel noted the word "us." *It's like they're a couple already*, she thought.

Scott murmured his apologies too. The five of them sat down to enjoy a good time of fellowship. Both Scott and Dinah were bubbling over, and Rachel chastised herself more than once for begrudging them what she suspected was a romantic interest in each other.

"Your faces are glowing," Shirley said. "This is an answer to prayer."

Brian cleared his throat. "Dinah, there's a group at our Church for new Christians. It would be great if you'd come along."

"That would be awesome. Thanks, Brian."

Brian smiled then ducked his head, and appeared to be studying the contents of his sandwich. He turned to Rachel. "Did you know that some people think there shouldn't be any hymns at altar call, and some even think that there shouldn't be an altar call at all?"

Brian's words caused a lively debate between him, Rachel, and Shirley, when Rachel suddenly felt bad that Scott and Dinah were not joining in. She looked at them, only to find that they were deep in conversation yet again. As Rachel was discussing another theological point with Brian and Shirley, Brian playfully tapped Rachel on the shoulder and said, "We'll have to agree to disagree."

Rachel laughed. At that moment, Scott looked up and caught Rachel's eye. He seemed none too pleased.

Why did he look at me like that? Rachel wondered, completely perplexed.

Everyone helped Shirley clear the table, but just as they reached the kitchen, Rachel recognized the familiar ring tone of Scott's cell phone. Scott left the room to speak. When he returned, he said, "Sorry, I have to leave, I'm afraid. A show dog breeder just called; her West Highland White had one pup but the labor stalled and it looks like I'll have to do a caesarean right now."

"What a shame, dear; I was hoping you'd stay for dinner then come with me to the afternoon service."

"Sorry Mom, gotta run.'"

Rachel thought for a moment. Scott had just recommitted his life to Jesus Christ and so would need all the Church time he could get at this stage. "Scott, I'll go. You stay here and go to Church with Shirley."

Scott looked as if he was about to argue, but Shirley laid her hand on his arm. "Would you, mind, Rachel? It's an awful imposition."

"No, that's fine, truly, Scott."

Rachel arrived at the surgery to find Linda was already there and had prepped the dog for surgery. The distressed owner was wringing her hands in the waiting room. The procedure proved more difficult than usual, but Rachel managed to save four puppies, three girls and one boy. The owner was delighted.

All the puppies needed resuscitation, and the mother dog had a bad reaction to the anesthetic, so Rachel had to wait some time before she felt that the mother dog and puppies could leave with their relieved owner. After she sent Linda home, she texted Scott to tell him how the surgery went, but he did not text back.

Just as Rachel was leaving the clinic, another lady hurried into the surgery with a cat, saying that the cat had been bitten by a snake while playing with it. Rachel thought from the description that the snake sounded like the common garter snake, but the owner insisted that the culprit was a timber rattlesnake. Rachel examined the cat, which was showing no sign of snakebite, venomous or otherwise.

After Rachel sorted out the cat, which was duly sent home with his owner, two different sets of people called in to purchase products as they saw that the clinic was open.

By the time Rachel got home, she was thoroughly exhausted, and headed straight for the bathroom. She ran a bath and poured in a liberal amount of grapefruit and bergamot bubble bath. When the bath was half full, Rachel decided she needed a stronger scent, so added a generous serving of French Lavender bubble bath.

Rachel lay in the bath for ages, letting the hot water soothe her aching shoulder and neck muscles, and scooping up the bubbles that threatened to overflow the bath. Rachel checked her cell phone again, but still no text from Scott. Rachel got the phone a little wet while checking it for texts, so tried to dry it, but then nearly dropped it in the bath. She threw it to safety, and to her relief it landed on the edge of the thick shag bath rug, away from the tiles.

Try as she might, she could not get Scott out of her head.

Was I imagining his attraction to me? she wondered. *He sure seems attracted to Dinah.*

Rachel hopped out of the bath and dried herself on her big, fluffy towel, and then rubbed on organic raw shea butter. Deciding she needed more of a perfumed scent again, Rachel lathered herself with orange blossom and honey body lotion. "I feel almost human again," she said aloud, as she dressed in her fluffy, blue bath robe. While she was looking for her fleece lined, Snuggie slippers, she came across the big, puffy, novelty Christmas Santa slipper socks that Dinah had given her for a bit of laugh, so decided to wear them. Rachel was about to dry her hair, when she had a horrible thought. Dinah! How would she get home? She hadn't thought about it earlier when she'd offered to take Scott's place at the clinic.

Rachel went into the living room. "Mom, is Dinah home yet?"

Carole looked up from her women's magazine. "No, she called to say she'd be late. Oh Rachel, don't get around like that! Your hair's all over the place, and your skin's all red and shiny, and whatever are those truly ghastly things on your feet?"

"Mom, no one's going to see me. I'm about to dry my hair; I was just worried about how Dinah was getting home."

Just then, Rachel heard the front door open.

Thank goodness - Dinah - I hope she's not cross with me for abandoning her. She must have gone to the night service with Shirley.

As Rachel reached the front door, Dinah walked through, with of all people, Scott. They both looked at Rachel, and laughed. "Nice Santas," Scott said, and then laughed.

Rachel put her hand to her hair, embarrassed.

I must look a fright, she thought.

Scott said goodbye to Dinah and Rachel, then he and Dinah hugged. Rachel was struck to the pit of her stomach with jealousy. Dinah, on the other hand, was very exuberant, humming a praise and worship song as she took Rachel by the arm. "You smell overpoweringly like a bed of flowers," Dinah giggled. "Come on, let's have some hot cocoa."

Sleep eluded Rachel that night, as she tossed and turned for hours, replaying Dinah's remarks about how nice and helpful Scott was.

And it shall come to pass, if thou shalt hearken diligently unto the voice of the LORD thy God, to observe [and] to do all his commandments which I command thee this day, that the LORD thy God will set thee on high above all nations of the earth:
And all these blessings shall come on thee, and overtake thee, if thou shalt hearken unto the voice of the LORD thy God.
(Deuteronomy 28:1-2)

Chapter Sixteen.

As soon as she arrived at work the next day, Rachel immediately noted that Scott was happy and in high spirits. He greeted her in an animated manner. Rachel did her best to return his greeting. She had concluded in the early hours of the morning that Scott and Dinah may only have feelings of friendship for each other. *Wishful thinking perhaps*, she thought.

"Rachel, are you okay? You haven't answered."

"Oh sorry. I was a million miles away. What did you say?"

"I said that Kenneth and I were going to a lecture this afternoon on the recent advances in lameness and diagnostic imaging of the competition horse, but Kenneth can't go now."

Kenneth smiled ruefully. "My sister's coming to town for Christmas and I have to meet her at the airport. She only changed her schedule last night. If you go in my place, Rachel, I'll take over your workload here for the day."

Rachel looked doubtful, but Scott prompted her. "The clinic has already paid for two people. I thought you'd be interested in the latest in lameness diagnosis."

"I am."

"It's settled then. We have to leave soon; it's in Duluth. Is there anything you need to do before we go?"

Rachel shook her head. *Only collect my wits and try not to be stressed that I have to sit next to Scott for a few hours' drive*, she thought.

As soon as they had pulled out of the parking lot, Scott took a fleeting look at Rachel. "Thanks so much for taking my place at the clinic yesterday; that was really good of you."

"That's fine; I didn't mind."

"I'll make it up to you."

"Oh no, there's no need," Rachel said half heartedly, wondering if he was going to offer her an afternoon off at some point.

"How about I take you to dinner?"

"Dinner?" Rachel could not believe her ears. She quickly recovered herself. "Oh yes, that would be lovely, thank you." The thought of dinner with Scott set her heart fluttering.

It's not as if it's a date, she told herself. *It's just his way of thanking me for substituting for him yesterday.* She thought a little harder. *If he's dating Dinah, or even attracted to Dinah and about to start dating her, then surely he couldn't have dinner with me, as how would that look?*

Rachel felt a headache coming on, and rubbed her temples.

Scott glanced at her. "Are you alright?"

"Yes, just a slight headache." *I would be alright if I could stop this internal dialogue; it's driving me to distraction*, she thought.

"I really appreciated you substituting for me; it was good I could go to the afternoon and night Church services. I needed that."

I'll bet you did, Rachel thought cattily, and then silently reprimanded herself for being so unkind.

Scott continued. "Dinah was a big help, in that I had just recommitted my life to Jesus, and she had just become a brand new Christian at the same time. It was wonderful that we were able to discuss things that only people in our circumstances could understand."

"Hmm," was all Rachel could manage to say out loud. *I hope he's not about to tell me that he's dating Dinah. Oh well, if he is, at least I'll know, and that will be good; it will stop me holding out false hope, and then I can get on with my life.*

Scott stopped at a red light. "I hope it didn't give the wrong impression."

Rachel's stomach muscles clenched. "What do you mean?"

"I think Brian is sweet on Dinah. I hope it didn't look like there was anything between me and Dinah, as that certainly isn't the case. We were talking as we had similar experiences, and we were sharing. We both helped each other quite a lot."

"Hmm." *I have to think of something to say*, Rachel thought, but she wasn't able to. Her thoughts were coming thick and fast. *Is this true? It must be; Scott wouldn't tell a lie. Unless he believes that and doesn't realize he's attracted to Dinah?*

Scott leaned over to look at Rachel, but just then the light went green, so he turned his attention back to the traffic. "I hope I haven't given Brian the wrong impression. I think he's attracted to Dinah, don't you?"

Too many thoughts were bombarding Rachel all at once. *Is Scott trying to find out if he has opposition for Dinah in Brian?* she wondered. *Surely not. Perhaps he's saying that to let me know there's nothing going on between him and Dinah, but that could just be more wishful thinking on my part.* The throbbing in her head got worse.

"Rachel, did you hear what I said?"

"Oh, sorry, Scott. Yes, I heard. Dinah and Brian have been friends for years. I didn't notice any obvious signs of attraction for Dinah from Brian," she answered truthfully. "But then again, I wasn't looking for it."

"I hope I haven't put my foot in it."

Rachel was puzzled. "What do you mean?"

"It's a bit awkward. It's none of my business; I shouldn't have said anything."

"I don't know what you mean."

Rachel looked at Scott's face. He was clearly uncomfortable. "I mean, if you are keen on Brian, I've put my foot in it by mentioning that I thought he was attracted to Dinah."

"No, I'm not!" The reply came out far more vehemently than Rachel had intended. "I'm certainly not attracted to Brian and never have been," she said in a more reasoned tone. "I don't know whatever could have given you that idea."

Scott did not reply, so Rachel looked at him again, and he was smiling.

Surely this means he likes me, she thought. *What other explanation could there be? Men! They're so confusing.*

Uncomfortable with the silence, Rachel added, "He's not my type."

Scott chuckled. "What is your type?"

Is he flirting with me? Rachel wondered. "Um, tall, strong, Christian, nice, animal loving, I suppose."

"Brian is all those things."

And so are you, she thought. Aloud she said, "Yes, I suppose so, but there's no chemistry between us."

Again, Scott did not answer, and Rachel battled with her thoughts all the way to the University of Minnesota Duluth, where the lecture was to be held.

"We've made good time; we're early," Scott said as he turned off the engine. "How about I buy us a coffee, to warm up?"

"Sounds good," Rachel said, her teeth chattering from the cold as a blast of frozen air hit her in the face, assaulting her senses. The cold air was immediately followed by a barrage of stinging sleet which pelted down on Rachel's face, causing her to tremble uncontrollably.

"You're frozen; would you like my coat? Duluth is known for being horribly, bitterly cold."

Rachel refused his offer, but then to her utter shock, Scott put his arm around her shoulders as they walked across campus to Kirby Plaza. He pulled her close, and she snuggled into him, breathing in his scent of wood pine, oak moss, and leather. Her heart was racing with excitement and delight. He only released her when they reached the warmth of the building.

The Northern Shores Coffee House was crowded, with every seat taken, and sitting outside was out of the question, given the weather which had now turned to a heavy snowfall. At any rate, the outdoor seating section was shut. Rachel was surprised to see that the Northern Shores Coffee House resembled an actual log cabin, despite being on the first floor of the building. The walls looked like logs, and the fireplace was surrounded by stone. The whole effect was comforting and cozy.

Scott and Rachel hurried over to the raging fire to warm up while they looked around for a vacant seat, when, much to Scott and Rachel's delight, the people sitting at the sofa directly in front of the fire left. Scott and Rachel immediately sat down before someone else could claim the seat. It was a little two seater sofa, which forced them to sit close to each other.

Within ten minutes, both were drinking coffee, Rachel with her hands wrapped around the cup to keep them warm.

Scott leaned back and smiled at her. "What's in your coffee?"

Rachel returned his smile. "It's a latté with caramel and chocolate mixed through, and topped with whipped cream and caramel and chocolate drizzles. What's in yours?"

"Well, it's a Snow Storm Mocha, and it's a latte with white chocolate; it's also topped with whipped cream as you can see, and these are toasted coconut flakes on the top."

Rachel screwed up her nose. "I don't like coconut."

"Okay, I'll remember never to cook anything for you with coconut in it, then."

Rachel stared at Scott, wondering if she should attach any importance to his words, or whether it was just a throw-away remark. He smiled at her, then tucked into his bagel and cream cheese. Rachel nibbled on her peanut butter chocolate chip muffin, deep in thought. She had prayed for a husband, and more so every Christmas when she looked at happy couples and felt alone, but a husband had never shown up. Was God finally answering her prayer?

*"For if ye forgive men their trespasses, your heavenly Father will also forgive you:
But if ye forgive not men their trespasses, neither will your Father forgive your trespasses."*
(*Matthew 6:14-15*)

Chapter Seventeen.

Rachel had not heard so many technical terms since she had left college. She was busy staring at a dorsomedial-palmarolateral oblique radiographic view of a competition horse's right front foot, when she felt Scott tense up beside her. She looked up and saw that a woman at the front of the seminar had stood up, and was leaving the lecture room.

The lecturer, who had a dry style and spoke in a monotone, droned on about extra-articular non-displaced incomplete fractures, and continually emphasized the need for the routine use of oblique projections in horses with foot pain. Rachel felt herself nodding off to sleep, when Scott elbowed her. "Coffee break time. Were you asleep?" He looked amused.

"Yes, well it's amazing how some people can make the most interesting subjects seem so boring." Rachel shot a furtive look at the lecturer.

Scott simply nodded, and Rachel followed him to a side room where coffee and cookies were provided. Many of the people seemed to know each other, and were standing around in groups chatting. An elderly man hurried over to greet Scott, and although Scott introduced Rachel, the man ignored her and spoke exclusively to Scott. Rachel drifted away and stood by herself by a window, sipping her coffee and watching the snow. The lecturer singled her out for his attention, to Rachel's dismay.

Rachel was listening to the lecturer tell her, in his monotone, all about the distal border fragments of the navicular bone. She sighed inwardly, and tuned out, looking around the room for something, anything, to catch her interest.

At that moment she saw the woman again, the one who had made Scott tense up briefly in the lecture. She was striding purposefully toward Scott. The woman was tall, and strikingly attractive, with long dark, wavy hair and a voluptuous figure. Unlike Rachel who was dressed for work, as were most of the other attendees, this woman was dressed more like Dinah usually did, in heels and a figure-hugging dress.

The woman touched Scott on the arm. They were too far away for Rachel to hear what was said, but the woman said something to the elderly man who left. She appeared to be speaking urgently to Scott, who crossed his arms and looked quite tense.

A man announced that the second part of the lecture was about to start, and asked everyone to return at once to the lecture hall. Rachel returned alongside the lecturer, who was still talking to her, and noticed that Scott and the woman were not making any attempt to move but were still deep in conversation.

Rachel sat with a knotted, clenched stomach through the second part of the lecture, and Scott did not return to his seat next to her until the closing minutes of the lecture. He did not make any attempt to explain his absence. However, instead of sitting close to Rachel with their arms touching, as he had in the first part of the lecture, he kept his distance.

When the lecture was over, there was no sign of the mystery woman, who had not returned to the lecture, and Rachel headed straight for the parking lot. Once in the car, she sighed deeply.

"Is everything all right?"

Rachel fastened her seat belt and looked at Scott. "Yes. I don't mean to sound ungrateful, but I was thinking that I should have waited 'til the paper was published, rather than attend in person."

Scott burst out laughing. "You and me both. Lunch?"

Rachel looked at the sleet which had increased in ferocity and was bombarding the windshield, sounding like a thousand urgent woodpeckers. "Should we wait 'til the sleet eases a little before going back into the building?"

"Oh no, not here," Scott said, "somewhere else. We'll drive for a while and find a restaurant on the way back. I don't want to run into... well, anyone who'll talk for ages," he finished lamely.

Scott drove for a while before he pulled over outside a timber building. "I ate here once, some time ago, with Kenneth, and the food was good. Let's hope it still is."

Rachel slipped on the icy pavement, and Scott took her arm to support her. "I bet you're pretending to slip just so I can take you in my arms," he joked.

Rachel caught her breath at Scott's words. Once again, she took in his masculine scent and fought the urge to lean closer to him. He did not release her arm until they were inside the restaurant. Rachel was excited to be spending some more alone time with Scott. Perhaps this would give her a better idea of how he felt about her.

The restaurant had both tables and booths, and Rachel was pleased when Scott led her to one of the booths. This was more private and intimate. The booths were down the length of one wall, and while the tables were next to them, there was no one in the immediate vicinity.

This is almost like a date, Rachel thought.

She loved the timber and leather look, and the amber lighting afforded the place a romantic ambience.

"The booths are a little tight. I'd better not eat too much or I'll never get out."

Scott laughed. "It's all right for you, being so slender. It's a bit cramped for me."

Rachel thought back to the mystery woman's voluptuous figure. *I wonder if he prefers tall, curvy women?* she thought.

The service proved to be quite efficient as a waiter immediately appeared at their table, although he clearly expected them to order without wasting any time looking at the menus. After thinking of the mystery woman, Rachel had lost some of her appetite, so ordered the half sandwich and a cup of soup. The soup was Manhattan shrimp and clam chowder, and the waiter assured her that it was not too spicy. For the half sandwich, Rachel ordered corned beef but the waiter repeated the order as roast beef. Scott was about to object but Rachel shook her head at him; she really didn't mind.

Scott ordered a large rib eye steak with onion rings, baked potatoes, crispy fries, and rice.

That's a lot of fat and carbs, Rachel thought. *It's a wonder he's so athletic-looking.*

As soon as the waiter had left, Scott addressed Rachel. "Sorry I missed the second half of the lecture."

Rachel did not know what to say, so mumbled incoherently and looked at the painting on the wall.

"I suppose you're wondering who the woman was."

Rachel again did not know what to say, so simply shrugged and hoped her outright enthusiasm to find out more about the woman was not written all over her face.

Scott squirmed in his seat. "That was actually Olivia, my ex-fiancée."

Rachel felt her jaw drop open in shock.

Scott rubbed his chin. "I haven't seen her since the break up. Although she's a vet in this state, she never goes to seminars. It was quite a shock to see her today."

Rachel felt a little nauseous. She hoped Scott wasn't pining after Olivia. At college, a close friend of Rachel's had fallen in love with a man who was pining after his ex-girlfriend to the extent that it made him afraid of commitment. They dated for a year, but he did want not want to get married. Her heartbroken friend finally broke it off when he eventually admitted that he would always be in love with his ex-girlfriend. Rachel did not want to end up like her friend. Rachel looked up and saw Scott was looking at her, so felt she should say something. "Didn't you say she got married?"

"Yes, but that's it. She said she wants a divorce."

It's going from bad to worse, Rachel thought, *she'll get a divorce and then she and Scott might get married.*

Scott was still speaking. "Yes, she wanted my advice."

"On whether to get divorced or not?"

Scott nodded.

That would be right, Rachel thought with dismay, her heart sinking. *Olivia must have wanted to know if Scott had feelings for her, so they could pick up where they'd left off.*

Scott appeared oblivious to Rachel's discomfort. "We haven't kept in touch. She had no idea that I'd fallen away from God for some years, or that I'd recently recommitted, of course. Her husband was in the ministry, so he doesn't want to get divorced, but she said they have continual fights due to his unreasonable jealousy and she's asked him for a divorce. She wanted some good, Godly advice."

"Oh." Rachel felt she should say something more substantial than "oh," so added, "And did you give her good, Godly advice?"

"I hope so. I told her to speak to a Pastor, but she said it wasn't the same as speaking to a friend. She told me a few years' worth of her troubles in an hour."

"Goodness me."

"Yes, and I don't think I was much help. I just quoted a lot of Scriptures."

"That's probably the best thing you could have done."

"S'pose." Scott looked doubtful.

At that point the food arrived, so the two ate their meals amidst happy conversation. In fact, they talked for some time after finishing lunch.

By the time Scott got Rachel home, it was quite late. He escorted Rachel to the door, and both of them laughed when she slipped yet again on the ice, right at the door. Scott gently pulled her into his arms. She felt herself go a little limp in his arms and her head rested on his shoulders. He placed a finger under her chin and tilted her head slowly until her lips met his in a warm, tender embrace.

*[A Song of degrees.]] I will lift up mine eyes unto the hills, from whence cometh my help. My help [cometh] from the LORD, which made heaven and earth.
(Psalm 121:1-2)*

Chapter Eighteen.

Rachel walked out of the treatment room, scratching herself. She had just administered a flea tablet to a dog, advised the owner that the tablet would kill all fleas on the dog between thirty minutes and four hours, and told the owner that the treatment must be repeated monthly. The poor dog was crawling with fleas, and Rachel felt quite itchy at the thought of it.

She escorted the owner to the door, squirming and scratching, her imagination working overtime. Just the thought of fleas was enough to make her think they were crawling all over her. At that moment, a familiar face pushed past her and hurried over to Linda, demanding to speak to Scott. Rachel did not hear the rest of the conversation but Linda hurriedly escorted the woman into Scott's office.

Rachel realized where she had seen the woman before; she was Olivia, Scott's ex-fiancée. She had no time to contemplate the significance of Olivia's visit, for her next patient was already waiting, an elderly dog with arthritis.

After she treated the elderly dog, Rachel walked out to check her next patient with Linda. At that moment, Cindy ran in, frantic.

"Quick, there's been an accident."

Linda and Rachel ran outside, and saw Olivia lying sprawled on the ice, her ankle twisted at a funny angle. Her face was contorted with pain and she was whimpering.

"A nasty break for sure, by the looks of it," Rachel said to Linda. "Quick, run inside and get Scott and bring some blankets."

Scott ran out, his face white. He fussed over Olivia and carried her back inside the clinic and Linda covered her with blankets. "Linda, Olivia's slipped in the ice in her unsuitable footwear." His voice held a lecturing note. "I'm going to take her to the hospital. Can you reschedule appointments?"

"Sure."

Olivia's face was white with pain. "I'm sorry; it's those stupid shoes," she said to no one in particular.

"Rachel, can you bring my car around to the front?" He tossed her the keys.

When Rachel drew the car up as close as she could to the front door to the clinic, Scott carried Olivia to the car and he and Rachel quickly made her as comfortable as they could. Scott slapped his forehead. "Oh, I forgot. I was supposed to meet Dinah this afternoon for coffee. Rachel, could you call and tell her I can't make it? Tell her what's happened." With that, Scott got in the car.

Rachel went back inside the clinic, feeling quite anxious. Scott was meeting Dinah for coffee? Why hadn't Dinah mentioned it to her? For that matter, why hadn't Scott? If Olivia hadn't turned up out of the blue and had a fall, she wouldn't have heard about this latest turn of events.

Surely Scott's not a player? she asked herself. *One day he kisses me and then soon after has coffee with Dinah. What's going on? This is just not right.*

She walked back inside and said to Linda, "Could you please hold my next patient for just a couple minutes? Scott asked me to call my sister Dinah and cancel their appointment this afternoon. It'll only take a minute."

Linda looked slightly embarrassed. "Oh I'm so sorry; I've only just called her now to cancel, and now I'm working on rescheduling Scott's clinic appointments. I'm sorry if I did the wrong thing."

"Not at all, that's fine, Linda." Rachel thought about the situation. *I won't mention to Dinah that I know that Scott was having coffee with her today and I'll see if she mentions it to me.*

"And, having made peace through the blood of the cross, by him to reconcile all things unto himself; by him, [I say], whether [they be] things in earth, or things in heaven. (Colossians 1:20)

Chapter Nineteen.

Rachel was exhausted. Try as she might, she only just managed to hold her drooping eyelids open. She'd been on the go ever since Scott had been looking after Olivia. She had taken on his patients today as well as yesterday, given the influx of emergencies, and she had taken his place on call the night before. Worse still, Dinah had not mentioned her coffee appointment with Scott at all.

Just after 4 p.m., Linda took her by the arm. "Rachel, you look beat. Go and take a quick nap on the sofa in the staff room. I'll call you if I need you."

Rachel protested, but Linda insisted. "You look asleep on your feet; it's just no good at all. Don't forget, people make mistakes when they're overtired. Kenneth can take your patients for the rest of the afternoon. Actually, so can Scott; he just called to say he's coming straight over. Go and sleep and I'll call you if there's an emergency." When Rachel went to speak, Linda held up her hand and added, "It's for the good of the patients."

"Well, since you put it that way." Rachel yawned widely. "I am having the most awful trouble staying awake. I can see why they use sleep deprivation as a torture."

"Off you go then." Linda waved her hand at Rachel as if she were shooing a naughty child.

As soon as Rachel lay on the sofa, she fell asleep, but woke herself up with a start when she snored loudly. Rachel sat bolt upright and looked around the staff room. Thankfully, no was there. Rachel always snored loudly when she was overtired. The clock on the wall showed that she had been asleep for almost fifty five minutes. Rachel lay back down and was wondering whether to try to catch a little more sleep, or check with Linda first. Just then she heard the door open. The high backed sofa was facing the window over the parking lot, so Rachel was unable to see who entered. She was about to sit up when she heard an angry voice yell, "How dare you!" so she instinctively ducked back down.

The next voice she heard was unmistakably Scott's. "Keep your voice down. This is a place of business and I won't have you causing any disruptions."

The angry voice continued, but was a little lower. "You won't silence me."

"Look, say all you like, just say it in a civil tone. What's all this about?"

"As if you don't know!" The voice was still angry but not as loud as previously.

"Why don't you tell me?"

Rachel could tell that Scott was annoyed but trying to stay calm. She debated whether to announce her presence, but figured that the time for that had passed, so decided that if they discovered her, she would pretend to be asleep. She felt bad for eavesdropping on the conversation, but felt there was no way she could show herself now. It would be horribly embarrassing for all concerned.

"You and Olivia, as if you don't know. Don't play games with me, Scott."

Scott's voice was tense. "There's nothing going on between me and Olivia."

The other man snorted rudely. "You took her to the hospital, and after she was discharged, you've been taking her food to her motel room."

"Well who did you expect would do it, if I didn't? You could thank me instead of accuse me, you know. You weren't here and Olivia has no family in these parts, as you well now. Someone had to do it."

"Well what was she doing here anyway, if not to see you?"

Rachel thought the man's tone belligerent and accusatory.

Scott took a deep breath. "She's very upset that the two of you have separated. She's spoken to her Pastor about it, but she thought she'd get my advice too."

The man sneered. "And what was your advice? Divorce me and marry you?"

"Jeremy, don't be ridiculous!" Rachel could tell that Scott was rapidly losing his patience. "I told her that you and she should have marriage counseling, and that it would be a good idea if you got anger management counseling."

"As if I'd believe that." Rachel thought that despite his words, the man seemed to be calming down. "Do you deny that you want her back?"

"That's absurd, Jeremy. Of course I don't want her back."

The man's voice sounded calmer now. "You haven't married all this time; I figured that was because you wanted Olivia back."

"I did at first, of course, when the two of you ran off together, but now I'm in love with someone else, not that it's any of your business."

"I'm sorry." The man sounded contrite.

Rachel however, was wondering at Scott's admission that he was in love with someone else. Dinah? Dinah was the one he was meeting in secret, but then he had kissed her, Rachel.

"Look, Jeremy, you really have to get this anger and jealousy under control. It's breaking up your marriage. Olivia said you refuse to get marriage counseling; why is that?"

The man sighed deeply and Rachel heard him take a few steps. She was worried he'd walk over to the window, but then the footsteps stopped and he spoke again. "Guilt, I suppose you could say."

"You mean that you were a married man and a Pastor, and you got involved with Olivia who was engaged to me, and had an affair with Olivia, and then divorced your wife and married Olivia." Although it all came out in one breath, Scott appeared to say it as a statement rather than a question. Rachel could not hear any resentment in his tone; rather, it seemed to Rachel to be a simple statement of fact.

Rachel did not hear Jeremy's reply, so assumed he must have nodded. Scott did not speak either, and the next voice Rachel heard was Jeremy's. "I can hardly tell a Pastor that."

"You mean your Pastor doesn't know your history?" Rachel could tell that Scott was taken aback by Jeremy's disclosure.

"Hardly." Jeremy sounded ashamed. "We changed denominations so the gossip wouldn't catch up with us. I wasn't about to tell anyone what we did. It was unGodly and unscriptural, and I felt that everyone would be looking at us funny all the time and judging us."

"The Pastor would have kept what you said in confidence."

"Sure, but I didn't want the Pastor to know I'd disobeyed God and had done what I did. What I did was terrible; I'm the first to admit it, and I'll also admit that I'm ashamed and I don't want anyone to know."

"Then why have you refused marriage counseling? That would be confidential, obviously."

"I didn't want to go to a non-Christian counselor, and I can hardly go to a Christian counselor for marriage counseling as I'd have to admit all sorts of things. I feel guilty for what I did; I don't know how to move on from it, and all that. I really don't need marriage counseling as I know it's not Olivia's fault - it's my problem to sort out first, and I can't see how without admitting what I've done."

Scott expelled a short, sharp breath. "Look, what's done is done. You can't go back now. This is quite a mess, Jeremy."

Jeremy sighed deeply. "I know."

"Well, if you won't speak to a Pastor, I'll give you some advice, from one Christian to another. The apostle Paul says to move forward. It's in Philippians. He says he forgets those things which are behind and he reaches forward to those things which are ahead. He says he presses toward the goal for the prize of the upward call of God in Christ Jesus."

"Yes, I know all that."

"And that doesn't help you?"

Rachel thought that Scott sounded perplexed.

"No. He was an apostle after all, and I'm, well, just me. There's no comparison."

"I see. So what you did was worse than what Paul did?"

"Yes, of course."

"Paul hunted down Christians and had them put to death."

There was silence for a while, then Rachel heard Jeremy speak. "You know, you'll think this strange, but I've never thought about it like that before."

"Jeremy, the Apostle Paul is not the only person in the Bible who messed up. King David had an affair with Bathsheba, a married woman, and he sent her husband to the front line to be killed. And Abraham told two separate kings that his wife was his sister. And there was Jonah who wouldn't listen to God, and Moses, who killed the Egyptian. Hey, even Joseph's brothers threw him down the well and sold him into slavery. I don't think what you did was quite as bad as that?"

Jeremy simply murmured, so Scott continued, "Well here's another Scripture for you, Jeremy. Jesus said, 'No man, having put his hand to the plough, and looking back, is fit for the kingdom of God.'"

Jeremy spoke up. "Yes, I can see what you say makes sense, but how to get rid of this guilty feeling?"

"With God's help, Jeremy. One of my favorite verses is the first six verses of Romans chapter eight. I have a Bible App on my iPhone." There was a scuffling sound, then Scott read, *"There is therefore now no condemnation to them which are in Christ Jesus, who walk not after the flesh, but after the Spirit.*

For the law of the Spirit of life in Christ Jesus hath made me free from the law of sin and death.

For what the law could not do, in that it was weak through the flesh, God sending his own Son in the likeness of sinful flesh, and for sin, condemned sin in the flesh:

That the righteousness of the law might be fulfilled in us, who walk not after the flesh, but after the Spirit.

For they that are after the flesh do mind the things of the flesh; but they that are after the Spirit the things of the Spirit.

For to be carnally minded is death; but to be spiritually minded is life and peace."

Rachel wondered how Jeremy would respond. She did not have long to wait, for he immediately said, "So are you saying I haven't been looking at this spiritually-minded? As then I'd have peace?"

"Pretty much," Scott said. "I'm saying you have been under condemnation, but no one is perfect in God's sight. Condemnation will keep us away from God. You need to admit what you did, repent, but then it is important to move on, with God's help. Put your eyes on God, not on man. The Bible is full of people who messed up, then became closer to God than they were before. I suggest you go and have a talk with your Pastor as soon as you can. I think you also should tell Olivia what you told me. I'm no counselor, but you've been living with this burden of guilt for so long, and that can't be good for a marriage."

Rachel heard muffled sounds, and wondered if Jeremy was hugging Scott. She heard the door open, and then close.

For God is not [the author] of confusion, but of peace, as in all the churches of the saints.
(1 Corinthians 14:33)

Chapter Twenty.

Rachel was sleep deprived. Although she'd had no more patients the previous night after accidentally overhearing the conversation between Scott and Jeremy, she was tired. Scott had insisted she take the day off, and Dinah had coerced her into going Christmas shopping with her. Rachel and Dinah had both done their Christmas shopping early this year, but both had a couple more gifts to buy.

Rachel kept yawning, but Dinah, on the other hand, was alert and happy, and chatted all the way to the Mall. "Let's have coffee first and then we can decide where to go first."

Rachel agreed, and Dinah steered her toward a sign that said, "Coffee House: Gourmet Coffee."

Dinah appeared to be ravenous. She ordered maple pecan granola with vanilla yogurt, a breakfast wrap with Swiss cheese, egg, tomato, spinach, onion, and mushroom, and a pumpkin spice, dark roast coffee. Rachel simply ordered a double shot skim latté in the hope that it would keep her awake.

"Rachel, you have to eat more than that. You can't exist on just coffee."

"Stop scolding; Dinah, you sound just like Mom." Rachel sighed and added, "I'm so tired. I can't eat when I'm tired. Anyway, how can you eat so much? You ate breakfast before we left."

"I'm in love and it's making me hungry!"

Rachel sat up to attention, adrenalin coursing through her. "What? You're in love?"

"I didn't want to say anything yet. Can you keep a secret?"

Rachel held her breath. "Yes of course, but why is it a secret?" She heard her voice come out in a stammer.

"Well, he was interested in someone else for a while, but then he realized his true feelings for me," Dinah gushed. "He's a bit embarrassed as this person still seems to think he's interested in her, so he wants to set her straight and he hasn't had an opportunity to have a good talk with her yet. He hasn't even told me who she is, but I promised I wouldn't say anything yet."

"Who is he?" Rachel could barely force out the words. Her chest tightened unbearably.

Dinah laughed. "Rachel, I just told you I couldn't say. I've already said too much. And no hints! Anyway, it should be obvious to you. Oops, that's a hint. Well, no more hints for you!" Dinah laughed again.

Rachel felt sick to the bottom of her stomach. It all made sense to her now. Scott was in love with Dinah.

Dinah clapped her hands in elation. "You know, this is the best Christmas ever. I have a wonderful man, and now I'm a Christian!"

Rachel could not help but smile at that. "True, and now we just have to work on Mom."

Dinah put her hand to her mouth. "Oh, how could I forget to tell you? Mom said she'd come to the Church Christmas party!"

Rachel was shocked. "You're kidding. How on earth did you get her to do that?"

"She was no trouble at all. She probably thinks it's a lost cause resisting now, with both of us Christians. I even caught her looking inside my Bible the other day, although she did close it fast and hurry out of the room when she realized I was looking."

"That's awesome news, Dinah." Despite the good news about their mother, to Rachel, the world was spiraling out of control.

*"And lo, the angel of the Lord came upon them, and the glory of the Lord shone round about them: and they were sore afraid.
And the angel said unto them, Fear not: for, behold, I bring you good tidings of great joy, which shall be to all people. For unto you is born this day in the city of David a Saviour, which is Christ the Lord."
(Luke 2:9-11)*

Chapter Twenty One.

The Wild Oak Animal Clinic was busy right up to Christmas Eve. Rachel was miserable, sitting on her bed early that morning, watching the snow fall gently out her window. *Father God, every Christmas I've asked you for a husband, and this Christmas You still haven't granted my wish*, she prayed. *I don't understand.* Rachel wept softy.

Rachel got up, blew her nose, and forced herself to have a shower. She was determined to put on a brave face so that she would not ruin Dinah's happiness.

After breakfast, the three women sat around the fire with their coffee mugs. Rachel had only had a sip of coffee when the doorbell rang. She motioned to the other two. "I'll get it."

"Who could it be?" her mother asked Dinah.

Rachel was wondering the same thing. She opened the door, and there, on the doorstep, covered in snowflakes, was

Scott. Rachel's stomach at once knotted up. "Come in; Dinah's by the fire."

"Dinah?" Scott looked utterly confused, and that in turn, confused Rachel. Nevertheless, she walked back into the living room, and announced, rather unnecessarily as he was standing behind her, "It's Scott."

Her mother and Dinah both greeted Scott, but Dinah remained seated. Rachel wondered why Dinah did not jump up and give Scott a welcoming kiss. The air grew a little tense.

"Err, Rachel, could I speak to you, please? In private," Scott added.

Oh dear, Rachel thought, *this is the talk, where he tells me he's no longer interested in me, and is dating Dinah. I'll just die of embarrassment, how awful.*

Rachel nodded sadly, and led Scott into the dining room. The dining room had a beautiful bay window which overlooked the banks of snow at the river. It was a bit too cheery for Rachel, given her present mood, so she led Scott through the double glass doors which separated the sun room from the dining room. There was no sun of course, it being the middle of winter, and so it matched Rachel's frame of mind perfectly.

Rachel noted that Scott looked awkward, so said, "There's no need to have a talk with me. I already know. I had a talk with Dinah."

Scott looked blank, and then confused. "Rachel, I have no idea what you're talking about, but do you mind if I say what I've come here to say? I'm a bit nervous about it."

"Okay then." Rachel was confused.

He's acting weird, she thought. *I could have saved us both some embarrassment. Looks like he's determined to tell me he's not attracted to me.*

Rachel felt tears forming, so stuck her fingernails into her hand hard, hoping the pain would somehow stop the tears that were now threatening to flow freely.

Scott reached into his pocket and drew out a little box. He handed it to Rachel.

Rachel took the little box and opened it. In it was an engagement ring. In a split second she knew it must have cost a fortune. Rachel knew about diamonds as her cousin Darlene had made her go shopping for an engagement ring with her about six months earlier. It had a huge diamond in the center with platinum filigree swirls holding the diamond, all in an art deco style. There was no hint of color and there were no eye-visible inclusions, which, if she remembered Darlene's words correctly, meant that the diamond was the highest quality. The sparkle and scintillation were such that she knew it had been cut to perfect proportions. She gasped at its beauty, but then had a moment's concern. She, Rachel, was the one who loved art deco and vintage items, not Dinah. Yet surely Dinah could hardly be disappointed with such a spectacular ring.

Rachel managed to find her voice with some difficulty. "Dinah will love it!" She hoped her tone did not betray her utter devastation.

Scott rubbed his forehead. "I must say, I wasn't expecting that reaction. You have me thoroughly confused. What does Dinah have to do with anything? Why on earth would I give her a ring?"

Rachel bit her lip. Her face flushed, despite the cold. Her head was spinning. "I'm the one that's confused. I thought you were going to have a talk with me to tell me that you're not attracted to me anymore and that you're in love with Dinah?"

"Dinah?" Scott looked shocked. "But Dinah and Brian are dating."

"Brian?" It was Rachel's turn to be shocked. "But why were you meeting Dinah in secret for coffee the day that Olivia had the accident?"

Scott stood for a moment, processing the information. "That wasn't a secret. Dinah and I both go to the New Christians group at Church; didn't she tell you?"

Rachel shook her head.

"I know I've been a Christian for years but I thought it would do me good to go to the New Christian group meetings as I've only just recommitted my life. Dinah wanted to get my advice about Brian. She's been attracted to him for years, but she'd heard that he used to date a lady from another Church."

Rachel was trying to take it all in. Everything seemed unreal, as if she were in a dream. "So, you're not in love with Dinah?"

Scott sighed, and then took Rachel by the shoulders. "No, Rachel, I'm in love with you. It was love at first sight for me. I want you to marry me. Now, I know you might think it's a bit soon, but we don't need to set a date yet."

Scott slid the ring onto Rachel's finger.

"My Christmas gift at last, thank you," she said softly.

"No, it's an engagement ring." Scott laughed. "You'll have your Christmas gift tomorrow."

Rachel, however, had been not been speaking to Scott, but to God.

With his hands on Rachel's shoulders, Scott pulled her to him. His lips were soft and caring. Rachel melted into him, thanking God with all her heart for His wonderful gift.

You may be interested in Kathleen Wiseman's ***The Morgan Brothers*** series (see details further on) and Historical Christian Romance series, ***Early Christians***.

Romans (Early Christians Book 1)

Julia is a young, wealthy, Roman woman living in Pompeii. Her life, dedicated to the pagan gods, is carefree. Her world is soon rocked, not only by the eruption of Mount Vesuvius which threatens everything she holds dear, but also by the arrival of the handsome Marcus, a convert to the new religion, a follower of Jesus. Can she escape not only the deadly eruption but also her mother's plan to marry her to the deceitful fish sauce merchant, Brutus?

Corinthians (Early Christians Book 2)

When Marcus and Julia finally locate Tiro and Paula in the city of Corinth, they find all is far from well. Tiro's aristocratic parents have arranged for him to marry the unscrupulous Lady Drusilla, who is eager to marry him to advance her social standing. However, Tiro's heart belongs to the servant girl, Paula. Can true love find a way? Or will Lady Drusilla's evil plans rule the day?

Ephesians (Early Christians Book 3)

Marcus and Julia travel to Julia's sister, Lucy, in the city of Miletus. Lucy asks them to escort her to Ephesus, where her beloved Quintus has settled after the destruction of Pompeii. Before they were abruptly parted, Quintus and Lucy had whispered words of love amidst the deadly lava of Vesuvius, so why is Quintus now betrothed to the Lady Livinia? What secret has torn Quintus and Lucy apart? Should Lucy put aside her feelings and settle for the pleasant Timothy? Or can God find a way where there is no way?

The Morgan Brothers Series.
Four books.

By His Grace (The Morgan Brothers Book 1)
Grace Elliot, under the advice of a family friend, broke her engagement to Daniel Morgan four years earlier as she did not want to be the wife of a Pastor. Now she has returned home to southern California from England due to her father's illness and intends to avoid Daniel at all costs. This proves to be more difficult than she thought, and his attempts to speak to Grace are thwarted by the beautiful Courtney. The dubious Jason Highfield is added to the mix. *By His Grace* is a sweet romance.

Caroline's Gift (The Morgan Brothers Book 2)
Caroline Elliot fancies herself as a matchmaker. Her handsome friend, the pastor Jeremiah Morgan, warns her not to meddle with love, but his warnings fall on deaf ears. Her latest attempt to play Cupid for her new friend Sarah Meade has gone amiss in more ways than one.
Will Caroline find true love, or she is destined to remain single forever?
Will her gift of matchmaking ruin her one true chance at happiness?

That Which Is Secret (The Morgan Brothers Book 3)
Courtney Blunt and Ezra Morgan are in love, but before he met Courtney, Ezra became engaged to Abby Bradford, now a missionary in Africa. While Abby no longer wants the engagement, for reasons of her own she refuses to break it. A heartbroken Courtney flees to Australia. How will the dangerous Australian outback bring her true love?

A Mustard Seed (The Morgan Brothers Book 4)
When Emma Barrett's husband was taken from her one dark, fateful night, she thought she would never find love again. That was, until Nehemiah Morgan came into her life. Is God offering her a second chance at love? Or will the contents of a safe deposit box tear them apart?

* * * * * * * * * * * * * * * *

John 3:16

"For God so loved the world, that he gave his only begotten Son, that whosoever believeth in him should not perish, but have everlasting life."

* * * * * * * * * * * * * * * *

Romans 10:9

"That if thou wilt confess with thy mouth the Lord Jesus, and shalt believe in thine heart that God hath raised him from the dead, thou shalt be saved."

* * * * * * * * * * * * * * * *

For automatic entry to all book giveaways, follow me on Facebook at https://www.facebook.com/KathleenWisemanChristianRomanceAuthor

Kathleen Wiseman loves to hear from her readers.

Follow her on Twitter: http://twitter.com/CleanRomanceBks

Follow her on Pinterest: http://pinterest.com/kathleenwiseman

Website: http://christianwomensfiction.com/

Facebook Page: https://www.facebook.com/KathleenWisemanChristianRomanceAuthor

Bonus Recipes

Note from Kathleen: *I hope you enjoy these Christmas recipes. They have been passed down from my great grandmother.*

German Black Forest Cherry Christmas Cake

2 Chocolate Sponges

Ingredients

3 eggs

3/4 cup sugar

1 cup self raising flour

3 tablespoons water

1 heaped tablespoon cocoa

Method

Preheat oven to 355 degrees F (180 degrees C)

Grease two 9 inch (22 cm) shallow round cake pans and dust with flour

Separate egg whites from yolks

Beat whites until stiff

Add sugar slowly and beat well

Add yokes and beat until thick

Fold in sifted flour and cocoa

Add water

Stir lightly and quickly

Pour into pans

Bake in oven for 15 minutes

Cool in pan for 5 minutes

Turn onto cooling rack

Cherry center

Ingredients

1 can (15 oz) (500 gr) Black Cherries in Kirsch

1 rounded tablespoon corn starch

1 tablespoon lemon juice

Method

Blend corn starch with 2 tablespoons cherry syrup (taken from the can) in saucepan on heat until thickens.

Place aside to cool

Buttercream Frosting

Ingredients

1/2 cup butter, softened

1 cup sifted confectioners' sugar

1/2 teaspoon vanilla

Method

Beat the butter and confectioners' sugar to a cream

Then add vanilla

Assemble the cake

Put cooled cherry mixture on both of the sponges, and then put them together

Put buttercream all around the outside

Beat 10 ounces (250 mls) of pure cream

Beat cream until stiff and add 1 tablespoon of sifted confectioners' sugar

Add 1 teaspoon of vanilla

Beat until stiff and then heap on top of cake

Take a 3 ounces (85 grams) bar of plain dark chocolate and peel with a swivel vegetable peeler to make it curl

Place the chocolate curls over the cream on sides and top of cake

Decorate the top of the cake with 15 maraschino cherries.

Traditional English Christmas pudding

This is best made several weeks before Christmas, and then hung in a pudding cloth in a cool, dry place.

Ingredients

20 oz (500 gr) currants

20 oz (500 gr) sultanas

10 oz (250 gr) raisins

2 oz (60 gr) candied citron peel

(125 gr) sliced, blanched almonds

20 oz (500 gr) butter

20 oz (500 gr) brown sugar

8 eggs

3/4 cup brandy

10 oz (250 gr) soft bread crumbs

10 oz (250 gr) plain flour

1 pinch salt

1 teaspoon baking soda

1/2 teaspoon grated nutmeg

2 teaspoons mixed spice

Method

Clean and prepare all the fruit

Cut the citron peel finely

Boil a very large pan of water

Cream butter and sugar

Add well beaten eggs and bandy

Stir in all the fruit and mix thoroughly

Add breadcrumbs and sifted flour with salt, soda, nutmeg, and spice

Mix well together

Place in a very strong pudding cloth, and tie with a string, allowing room for it to swell

Place in boiling water and cook for 6 hours

Hang in a cool, dry place

Serve

Steam as above for a further 3 hours on the day it is to be eaten, OR simply slice it and heat individual slices in the microwave.

Serve with Brandy Butter (see recipe below) or double cream OR dress with warm brandy which is set alight, and then may be served with double cream.

Brandy Butter

1 heaped cup butter (softened)

2 cups sifted confectioners' sugar

4 tablespoons brandy

Mix ingredients until smooth.

Printed in Great Britain
by Amazon.co.uk, Ltd.,
Marston Gate.